I0676164

THE LUST LIST: MILES RIOT

STRINGS ATTACHED

MIRA BAILEE

NoMi Press

Euphoria Publishing
NoMi Press
www.euphoriapublishing.com

Publisher's Note: This is a work of fiction. Names, characters, places, and incidents are a product of the author's imagination, and any resemblance to actual people, living or dead, or to businesses, companies, events, institutions, or locales is completely coincidental.

ISBN-13: **978-0692618868**
ISBN-10: **0692618864**

Printed in the United States of America

For anyone who's a fan of

~~*sex, drugs, and rock and roll*~~ *LOVE*

Chapter One

Abby

We're in Memphis tonight, playing a show at The Rockwood, a beautiful venue with a vintage look to it. Though we're in another city, I feel like we're in another world. It might look the same—Kennedy's seducing the audience with her vocals, the guys are keeping the energy high and the music loud, the crowd is going wild every time a new song begins—but the air is different. The electricity between me and Miles has shifted. Not in a bad way. It's just more...real. I know him more now, all his dark secrets, and I feel the need to protect him however I can.

Of course, his sister Kennedy feels the same way, wanting to protect her big brother, and since he went out of his way to come get me back in Texas, she resents me being around that much more.

"You're a risk," she told me on the tour bus earlier. "You two won't last, and one minor grudge will have you turning on him in a second."

Sorry, hon. You don't know me that well. There may be no guarantees about my relationship with Miles, but I take pride in my integrity, and Miles will always be safe with me. Little does she know, he told me everything. About his jail time, his probation, how—if the tabloids find out—he and the band are utterly screwed. I'm trying to turn my nerves to steel as I anticipate tonight's conversation. We have to come up with a plan to get *Scandal-Lust* off Tempest Ultra's back, and by *we*, I mean Kennedy and I have to be in the same room working together. Call me thrilled...

*

My tall, sexy man comes straight to me after the show, pushing me against the closest wall and kissing me hard. I grab on to the waistline of his jeans, savoring the intense heat emanating off of him. Post-show, sweaty, adrenaline-rushed Miles is almost too hot to handle.

"This is my favorite part of being on stage," he says quietly into my ear. His warm breath on my skin sends a chill down my spine.

"But you aren't on stage anymore." I laugh and kiss his exposed neck.

"Aren't you a smartass?" He steps back and checks me out, head to toe. Tonight, I'm not trying to fit into the rock crowd. I'm wearing a thin sundress and an old favorite pair of brown boots I found in my closet at my mom's house. This small town girl knows who she is—and what she wants. "Don't expect that dress to stay on long tonight," he says.

Miles is shoved from behind as Kennedy walks past. He hardly budges but rolls his eyes. "I've been dealing with that attitude since the day she was born." He looks down at me. "You ready?"

Not at all. I'd much rather keep a healthy distance between me and that rock princess. "Let's go."

We follow after Kennedy to a backstage warm-up room. No one else is in there, and Miles locks the door behind us.

"I hope you aren't in here to ruin my mood," she warns, surveying herself in the mirror and smoothing her smudged eyeliner.

"We have to talk about this issue with *ScandalLust*," Miles says, sounding very confident.

Kennedy spins around toward us. "Maybe later. Listening ears cause problems."

"She already knows."

"Knows what?" Kennedy's eyes go wide, and she crosses her arms in front of her chest.

"Knows everything down to my real name."

There's a second of a pause, and I can practically see the steam building up in Kennedy's head. "Are you out of your fucking mind, *Matthew*?" she yells at him, the name he was born with sounding like a foreign word. Kennedy doesn't even look at me. It's like I'm not in the room. "You going to start telling every woman you screw?"

"I'm only screwing one woman, thanks." His bluntness makes me blush. "She's not working with *ScandalLust*—"

"Yeah, right."

"She's not. But she wants to make them think she is, so we can get them off our tail."

Kennedy finally turns my way, looking at me with obvious disgust. "My stupid brother may be dumb enough to trust you, but believe me. We don't need your help."

Miles steps closer to his sister. The authority he exudes is intimidating. Only his sibling would be stubborn enough to stand up to that. "Listen close. You have no say in this. The three of us are the only ones who know everything going on. We *will* work together and figure this out. Now sit your scrawny ass down and act like an adult."

We all sit down—Miles and I on the couch, Kennedy on the chair across from us. She's livid, but it's obvious she has no choice here.

"I've scheduled a meeting with them." I try to speak with self-assurance, but it's hard with Kennedy glaring at me. "It's in two days, when we're in Atlanta. They think I have the proof they want for their story."

* * *

Miles

"How many people are showing up?" Kennedy asks, and I'm surprised to hear my sister sounding almost civil.

"I'm not sure," Abby says. "Two? Polly, the executive editor, and maybe one of the other writers will be there. That's all I know. There won't be any cameras. They've assured me my part in this will be confidential."

"No cameras..." Kennedy's got an idea. She may act impulsively at times, but if anyone will have a surefire way of dealing with this, it'll be the queen of manipulation.

Next to me, Abby's bouncing her leg nervously. Was I wrong to bring her into all this? I don't know. I don't really care. My selfish instincts took over when I went after her in Texas. I wanted my girl back. She can handle my baggage.

"What dirt can we dig up on our friend Polly?" Kennedy asks, staring at Abby.

Abby raises an eyebrow in curiosity but then digs out her phone. She hesitates to respond as if she's unsure what Kennedy really wants, but as she scrolls through websites, she starts sharing information. "She's been married three times. Caught cheating with a camera man a couple years ago. She has an eight-year-old son. Went to school at—"

"What if we hit her where it hurts?" Kennedy interrupts.

Abby drops her phone into her lap. "What do you mean?"

"I mean," Kennedy shifts her irritated glare from Abby to me, "we take advantage of the no-camera situation and let Miles do what Miles does best."

"Care to elaborate?" I ask.

Her face is brightening. She's getting excited about this scheme. "Abby goes in first, scopes things out, and distracts the writer. You and I check the surroundings for any secret cameras because tabloid bitch is probably a liar. And once the coast is clear and Polly is all alone, you go in being all asshole-ish and tell her to back off. Use the information we found to prove we're keeping tabs on her. Tell her you'd really hate to see something happen to that little son of hers."

"You want me to threaten her kid? Because that'll do me a world of good for staying out of jail."

"It'll be her word against yours. Trust me, you'll be so convincing, she'll pack up and go home, forgetting Tempest exists."

It's official. My sister's insane. But...she has a point. This could be the only shot we have of getting to *ScandalLust* without a bunch of paparazzi recording the whole event.

"And what would I supposedly do to her boy?"

Abby tenses beside me. Kennedy shrugs. "Steal his lunch money." She laughs. "You could convince the kid his mom's a cheating liar and he doesn't know his real father—ooh, I like that."

"I think the subtle threat would be more effective. Let Polly be the one to think up all the possibilities," I say.

"Fine. But we should plot out what you'd hypothetically do, just in case you have to be more...persuasive."

Or maybe Kennedy just wants to immerse herself in this new game. "Whatever," I say. "So, Abby gets the writer out of the way. I'll get rid of any paps."

"What do you mean *get rid of*?" Abby asks, her body stiff and voice shaky.

"I'm not killing anyone, if that's what you're thinking. I'll just restrain them or—"

Before I can finish, she gets up and storms out of the room.

Kennedy shakes her head in disapproval. "I can't believe you told her. She can't handle this the way you and I can. She's going to screw everything up."

"I'll talk to her. It'll be fine." I get up and leave, passing Dax and Nate in the hallway.

"Looks like you pissed off your girlfriend again." Nate laughs.

I don't have time to talk to them about it, and neither of them knows about my past. It's just been safer that way. "Where'd she go?"

Dax points down the hall toward the exit door. I walk quickly out of the building and scan the sidewalk to my left and right. She's a few feet away, lit up by a streetlight, leaning against the wall of The Rockwood.

I start with the only argument I have. "You said there wouldn't be cameramen, so it's not going to be a problem."

Her shoulders drop in disappointment. She doesn't even look at me. "But if there *were* people there with cameras, you'd have no problem beating the crap out of them. Just like you have no problem threatening a woman and her *child*. Miles...I...That's..."

The woman who writes for a living has no words. I've really screwed up this time.

I sit on the ground next to her, my back against the wall. She drops down by my side. Inches between us feel like miles.

When she speaks, she sounds broken. Something's changed between us. My confession to her may have done more harm than good. "Miles, I won't judge you for your past. Everyone messes up, and you're paying the consequences. But lying. Manipulation. Violence. You're better than all that."

"I think you're the only person who feels that way."

"Well, how do *you* feel?" She leans against me, and her touch brings clarity. Everything will be all right.

No, I'm not a liar or a manipulator. I'm not perfect though, and when shit needs to get done, I'll do whatever's necessary. But I'm not telling Abby all that. The silence lingers between us.

"We have to find another way," she says.

Kennedy's plan would work. It's quick and dirty and gets the job done. *ScandalLust* would disappear. But at what sacrifice? Abby may have forgiven me for my past, but if I follow through, what will she think of me then? I have to prove I'm different from who I once was.

"We'll find another way."

Chapter Two

Abby

It's hard to remember the real world still exists. Between my feelings for Miles and the quiet storm brewing between us and *ScandalLust*, I've nearly forgotten I have a day job. That is, until my boss, Jonathan, texted this morning scheduling a 10:00 a.m. video conference.

"You really wanted to wake up early to talk to me?" I ask. Jonathan's become a good friend over the years. Not only is he a great boss, but he's like a brother who knows just how to push my buttons. It's all his fault I'm on a tour bus that just stopped in Atlanta an hour ago. I should thank him for it later.

"I arrived at the office when I thought, what's my rock star employee up to? You aren't leaving Lydian for a life on the road are you?"

Jonathan runs a hand over his scruffy chin. The hair on his face is the same length as the hair on his head, and his black-framed glasses make him look more like a college student than the editor-in-chief of a major magazine. He says his boyfriend prefers the look, and women who don't know he's gay seem pretty drawn to him as well.

I won't lie. When I started at Lydian Magazine, I had a little crush on him, but it was quickly smothered when Dee broke the news he wasn't into women.

I laugh at the memory. "Nah, I'll be back soon. But I do need to extend my week. I need a couple more days. That all right?"

His eyes narrow. "What's holding you up? It's not like you to miss a deadline."

"The article will be done. I just have a few things I need to wrap up before I come home."

"Uh huh. As your superior, I'm not going to ask you which band member has you all *wrapped up*. But I'd like my feature editor back here as soon as she can."

The camera shows every inch of the shock on my face. "Your feature editor? Are you forgetting I'm just a lowly staff writer?"

"See? That's where you're confused. You left L.A. a staff writer. But you've been gone so long, you missed your own promotion. Charles Jackson's last day was yesterday, and we unanimously voted you in to take his place."

I'm speechless. I love my job, but I've always assumed it was a placeholder until I got my dream job at Unwired Press in Dallas. Taking this promotion is basically a commitment to stay in California much longer than I want to. But feature editor, getting to organize the major content of our magazine? How can I say no to that?

"I don't know what to say."

"Don't worry about speaking. Worry about writing. I want that article from you." He shifts to friend-mode. "I'm really proud of you. Honestly, I had my money on you running back here by the end of day two on that bus."

"Wait. You guys have a pool going?" I'm not sure how to feel about that. Offended? Amused?

"Nah. That wouldn't be very professional. But if we *did*, I would've lost anyway. Good for you, sticking it out. It's your professionalism that's gotten you so far."

My cheeks warm. "Thanks. I really appreciate that."

"Yeah, yeah. Now get back to work."

He hangs up and the computer goes dark. A smile is glued to my face as I shut the laptop.

* * *

Miles

Abby's sitting on the couch, her feet propped up on the coffee table, as she finishes a conversation with her boss. I sneak a glimpse at her, her blond hair down around her shoulders, its red and black ends wispy and messy with curls. She's in a loose fitting white t-shirt and shorts that show off her long, tan legs. For the rest of the band, it feels ungodly early, but Abby is alert and energized as she focuses on her work.

It's incredibly sexy.

I hop down from my bunk and approach her. "Good morning, Ms. Professional. Can I be your naughty intern?"

She looks up at me with her bright blue eyes. "I don't know, sir. We'll have to schedule an in-depth interview."

I snatch her laptop, putting it behind me on a chair. Unwilling to keep my hands off her a second longer, I lift her up and lay down on the couch, pulling her down on top of me. Her thigh presses in between my legs, and I'm instantly hard. I grab fistfuls of her hair and pull her face to mine, our lips crushing together. Her tongue massages mine as my hands eagerly explore the curves of her body. I hug her tight, pulling her closer to me as I pull my mouth from hers.

"So do I get the job?"

She gives me a sexy half smile. "I don't know. I have to interview the rest of the candidates first."

I playfully push her. "Ouch. That's painful."

"To your sensitive heart?" She sits up straight again, stretching her legs across mine.

Sensitive heart, my ass. "My ego," I correct her, and she laughs.

"I'm being promoted at the magazine," she blurts out.

"Is that what that meeting was about?"

She nods. "You're looking at the new feature editor."

"Wait. What about your high hopes for that other magazine. That boring, country one."

"Don't describe my dream job as boring, mister! It'll have to go on hold though. This is a great opportunity, and I love Lydian Magazine."

"So you're staying in L.A. for good?" I didn't even think of it before, but if she left for that other gig, what would happen between us?

"I'll be there for a while longer. I'm not sure if *for good* is the right phrase."

I sit up and lean over to kiss her again, realizing how grateful I'm suddenly feeling. Okay. So maybe the sensitive heart thing is a little true. "Works for me," I tell her. "I wouldn't be able to let you go anyway."

She smiles, and then the expression on her face changes. She's back to looking like Ms. Professional again. "So we need to figure out a plan for *ScandalLust.* The meeting's tomorrow."

It's the last thing I want to talk about, but we should get it over with. "Do you have any ideas?" I ask her.

"One." She pauses, putting her words together before she speaks. "Why don't we tell them the truth?"

"The truth?" I sit up straighter, leaning forward, my elbows on my knees, while she tries to explain why this is a good idea.

"Yes, the truth. It's straightforward. It would be coming from you. And if you admit it was a huge mistake, it won't have the repercussions you're so worried about. Plus, being in a tabloid, most intelligent people won't give it the time of day, *including* Stone and Rev Records."

I stand up, shaking my head. This is unbelievable. "Did you not listen to a word I said? Or are you just out of your mind?"

"You don't have to insult me, Miles. The truth is a valid option."

"Maybe in your cookie cutter world. But it doesn't work for me. Why the hell would I even risk it with *ScandalLust*?" I glance up at the other bunks, making sure Nate and Dax are still asleep. I speak in a hushed—albeit pissed off—whisper. "You think saying sorry is enough to remove the consequences? That's insane. Those tabloid assholes would spin the truth into something even worse than it already is. They'd throw us all under the bus for their benefit. And at the end of the day, Tempest would be screwed. No record deal. No label. No career. If that's your best idea, we're going back to Kennedy's." I spin away from her and walk toward the head of the bus. Abby doesn't get it. She can't. She's too naive and...sweet. She doesn't understand the very real threat of losing everything we've worked for. She doesn't get that having the truth out there means all eyes on me, waiting for me to screw up—to violate my probation—so they can throw me back in jail. Fuck the truth.

I don't bother looking back at Abby. Yeah, I'm mad that her great idea is the worst one imaginable. She can sit there and think about that for a minute. I grab the bourbon from the liquor cabinet and pour some into a low-ball glass, but as soon as I pick it up to take a gulp, an alert on my phone starts beeping.

"Fucking dammit." I grab clothes from my bunk and quickly change.

"What's wrong?" Abby asks, standing up.

I try to stay mad at her, but it's hard. "I have a meeting."

She scrunches her forehead while I run my hand through my hair and shove my feet into shoes. I grab my phone and pull up the location—it's a ten-minute walk. I'll just barely make it.

"What sort of meeting?" she asks.

I give her a quick kiss on her forehead. "Anger management." Then I leave.

* * *

Abby

I try not to laugh that my boyfriend—who just threw a tantrum because he didn't like my idea—is on his way to anger management. Maybe the meeting will give him a chance to think rationally about what I said. Maybe he's not used to having to act like a real adult. Sometimes, doing the responsible thing is hard—but it's the *right* thing to do.

Outside the bus window, I see we're parked at the hotel we're sleeping in tonight. In the next hour or so, hotel staff will come get our things, taking them up to our room. I'm starting to get accustomed to this routine. Wake up in a new city. Have others take care of your needs. Be spoiled by high-end luxuries. This may not be the comfortable, small town life I love, but the spontaneity and adventure are growing on me.

I fix my hair and pull on my brown boots, deciding I shouldn't take the adventurous side of me for granted.

It's hot out, so I think an iced coffee is just what I need. I scan the busy street. Lots of shops and boutiques. Cafes and diners. We've got hours before tonight's show. I'm going to do some exploring.

I spend a good hour working my way down the strip, window shopping and going into stores that catch my eye. It's a peaceful, calming morning, until one shop clerk completely catches me off guard. I'm in a family-owned boutique looking at the most gorgeous earrings when I hear someone approach from behind me.

"Abby? Abby Clarke?" someone asks with a thick southern accent.

I turn around wondering how I can possibly run into someone I know way out in Atlanta, but the woman doesn't look familiar at all. She wears a black dress and her bright red hair is up in a bun on top of her head.

"I'm sorry. Do I know you?"

The woman is wide eyed, and when I ask my question, she bursts into a fit of giggles. "Of course not. I'm nobody special. I just can't believe you're in my store."

She's acting like I'm some sort of celebrity. I smile kindly. "Your jewelry is beautiful. I was just looking at these." I motion toward the dangling earrings.

"Oh, pick a pair. I want you to have them. That would be so amazing."

"Thanks, but that's not necessary. I want to buy them."

The woman laughs again. "There's no way I'm letting you pay for those. How about this? You take a picture with me, and that can be your payment."

My words come out a little harsh. "Why do you want a picture with me?"

She looks at me like I grew a second head. "Because you're Abby Clarke. You're dating

Miles Riot. *The* Miles Riot. Do you have any idea how lucky you are?"

Yeah, I'm pretty sure I think I do, but I'm not lucky just because he's a rock star.

She continues telling me all about myself. "You and Miles were just in *ScandalLust* looking like the cutest couple. How did that happen? I mean, he was with those other girls before—I've kept *every* article, so I know just *how many* women he's been sneaking around with." She giggles again. "But ever since he started seeing you, it's like he's *only* with you. You must have the magic touch. Can you tell me what he looks like na—"

"One photo. But then I really have to go." The fanaticism here is making me a little uncomfortable, so now I just want to leave.

She points to her jewelry display. "Pick your earrings, and if you get the chance, *please* wear them on the red carpet. Promise me you will."

I can't even think of a time when I'll be on the red carpet any time in the near future, but

I smile and nod. Anything to appease this Miles Super Fan.

She runs behind the counter, mumbling to herself. "I can't believe this is happening." She returns with her phone and throws her arm around my shoulders. I just remembered I didn't put on any makeup this morning.

"Let's keep this off the Internet, okay?" I know my request is useless. This will be uploaded the second I walk out of here. Oh well, she may have recognized me, but most people won't.

"Say cheese!"

She snaps the picture, and I graciously get the hell out of the store.

*

I wasn't ready for that confrontation. I still haven't had my caffeine. A few blocks down, I spot a coffee shop on the opposite side of the road. Walking fast, I shove the bag with the earrings down into my purse and do a quick look over my shoulder to make sure I'm not being followed by that store clerk. As excited as she was to see me, I can't imagine what she'd do if she followed me all the way back to the hotel and ran into Miles.

Hurrying into the coffee shop, I take one more worried glance back and then approach the counter.

"Medium iced caramel latte, please." I pay and move off to the side.

It's a cute coffee shop, one of those hangout places with a big couch and plush chairs. Bookshelves line one of the walls, and I scan the titles as I wait for my name to be called.

Once I get my drink, I find a quiet two-seater table and sit down, only now noticing the thrill running through me. Is this what it's like to be Miles Riot's girlfriend? Being recognized? Meeting strange fangirls? Having people looking at me through the eyes of *ScandalLust*?

I'm trying to convince myself the attention is awful, but I can't. I just want to be with Miles—moody, temperamental Miles with the hidden heart of gold. If the attention and weird interactions go with it, then I'll take it all.

I'm smiling to myself when the chair moves across from me. Startled, I snap my attention upward and see a man sitting down. He's wearing a blue polo shirt and black pants. His hair is kept short and his brown skin glistens with a sheen of sweat, like he was just outside. I don't see a camera, but that doesn't mean he isn't a pap.

"Excuse me," I say, trying not to sound as irritated as I feel.

"I'm so sorry to scare you. I didn't mean to. My name's Terrance Young. I was hoping we could have a chat."

"Are you with *ScandalLust*?" Now I don't hold back on my irritation. We have a meeting scheduled for tomorrow. They have no right to approach me beforehand.

"Oh, heavens no," he says. "Nothing like that. I just had a couple questions about Tempest Ultra. You're touring with the band, right?"

"I'm not going to answer that, nor am I going to tell you anything about them. Who are you?"

He disregards my question. "I'm not one of the bad guys, ma'am. Granted, intruding on your coffee hour probably didn't earn me any brownie points."

"To say the least."

He laughs, and I smile.

"So let me start over. I'm Terrance." He reaches across the table and shakes my hand. His delayed efforts at using his manners make me laugh.

"Abby," I reply.

"How are you liking Atlanta?" Terrance sits back in his chair, getting comfortable.

"It's all right, so far. I haven't been here long."

"There's an excellent diner two blocks that way." He points out the window. "All southern, home cooked food. I recommend the country-fried steak and mashed potatoes. The gravy they use—it's made from scratch and good enough to drink with a straw."

"I'll keep that in mind."

He nods with approval. "So the band—"

"I told you I won't talk about them."

He pauses, looking distant like he's thinking of another angle to push. Then he reaches into his back pocket, pulls out his wallet, and retrieves a business card. Handing me the card, he says, "I'll leave you to your coffee. I really didn't mean to bombard you. Next time you're in Atlanta, give me a call. I'll tell you where to find the best chocolate soufflé."

"I'll keep that in mind."

Terrance nods a goodbye and leaves the coffee shop. I return to my latte, feeling a little like a jerk. Did I jump to conclusions with that guy? Was he just being nice? Maybe he's a fan and just wanted to innocently talk.

I drop his card down into my purse, considering this and feeling bad. Oh well. I can call him sometime and apologize.

Chapter Three

Abby

From backstage, I have the perfect profile view of Miles as the band plays tonight's show. His tight jeans hug his ass just right. The black sleeveless shirt he's wearing shows off his muscular arms, and I watch a vein throb in his right arm while he plays his guitar. He steps closer to the mic to sing, and my eyes linger on his mouth. With his hair concealing most of his face, his mouth is all you can really see anyway, but I'm mesmerized as I watch his tongue wet his lips, as he opens his mouth to sing, as his sexy growl of a voice perfectly harmonizes with Kennedy's vocals.

I lift my phone and take a picture, texting it to Dee, along with the message,

How did this become my life?

I hit send and await her response, but then the double meaning of my message hits me.

How did this rock star gig become my life? How did touring become my life?

How did *Miles* become my life?

Watching him play, I can't ignore the way my heart skips a beat. My mind races with everything that's happened in such a short time. The song he wrote for me. The first time we slept together. The incalculable lust that explodes between us any time we're near each other. The way he opened up to me and told me his darkest secrets. How he makes my entire soul feel more alive.

I need him. And if I trust my own intuition, he needs me too.

My phone buzzes, and I look down.

I told you so.

If she only knew how hard I'm falling for this rock star of mine.

*

After the show, Miles and I walk hand-in-hand the six blocks down to a bar where the band is celebrating another great night.

"I'm sorry about this morning," he says out of nowhere.

A crowd of people follow behind us, but Miles and I are in our own world.

He continues, "It feels weird being back here. I lived here for a long time, and then everything happened and I had to disappear. So I'm just a little on edge. I shouldn't have snapped at you this morning."

Is this the anger management talking, or is this truly coming from him? "It's okay," I say. "You were right. The truth isn't going to work in our favor. Not with the tabloids." I still think it could, but knowing how resistant Miles is to the idea...I need to accept that there's a better strategy for dealing with them.

"We'll figure it out," he says, as though he read my mind.

The crowd of people behind us has caught up, and Miles amuses them by treating them all like old friends. He strikes up conversations, dodges personal questions in his own clever way, and lets them take photos with him. Celebrity Miles is incredibly sexy.

We get to the bar, and the rock star treatment doesn't stop there. Several people offer us free shots, raising their own glasses in a toast. The rest of the band catches up, staking a claim at one of the high top tables, and a bartender comes over with a pitcher of local craft beer and a handful of glasses. Miles takes a seat next to me, draping his arm around my hips. I notice the disappointed looks on the fangirls around us. One turns to whisper to a friend. Another gives me a dirty glare. I make eye contact with her and give her a big Kennedy-worthy fake smile. She spins on her heel and stomps away. But when another groupie walks up, I almost lose all my confidence. My breath catches in my throat.

Her red hair is instantly recognizable, though it's no longer in a neat bun on top of her head. She's got it down and around her shoulders in big waves. Her makeup is ten times darker, and she suddenly has a nose ring. The woman I met this morning in her shop is very different from the woman I'm looking at now, but her eyes still glisten with the same obsessive excitement. She claims a spot on the other side of Miles and leans in close.

"Great show tonight!" she says, loudly.

I'm trying to put on a polite face. "They *were* great. I'm glad you were able to make it. You must have closed shop early."

Miles is looking at us like he's missing the joke. "You two know each other?"

The girl starts to talk, but I interrupt her.

"We met this morning. She's a *big* fan of yours." I look at Miles with an expression meant to convey, *Careful, this girl's a little too enthusiastic about you.*

"I am. My name's Miley. Isn't that funny? Miles? Miley?" She giggles.

"Hilarious." Miles is more amused than irritated. He so clearly loves the attention of doting fans.

I'm getting a really uncomfortable vibe from this girl—Miley, now that I know her name—and I don't like how close she is to Miles. I'm not one to be possessive, and I trust Miles, but at this stage of our relationship, everything feels so vulnerable. Cracks in the foundation can send us into a downward spiral we can't recover from.

"So Miley," I start to say, but a hand grabs my shoulder, and I almost shriek. I spin around. It's Kennedy. "What?"

"We need to talk."

Suddenly, I'd much rather spend the evening hanging out with fangirl Miley.

I follow Kennedy back outside where she stops on the sidewalk just outside the door. "What did you tell Devon?"

Where did that come from? Why would I be talking to her boyfriend? "I haven't—what are you talking about?"

"Please, you're much too transparent to pull off my games. I get that you were mad at me about what I did to you and Miles, but that's over now. Why'd you have to keep it going and screw things up between me and Devon?"

"I told you I haven't talked to him. What's going on with you two?" *Besides everything.* They cheat on each other. They're always fighting. They break up and make up nonstop. I don't know why anyone would want to cling onto such a dysfunctional relationship.

"After he found out I lied to you and made me come clean, it's like he changed. Usually he stays mad for a day or so, and then he comes back to me. But he's not talking to me. Not answering his phone. I can't get back to

L.A. right now, but it's obvious he's not coming out here. The only reason he'd stay mad this long is if someone convinced him to."

"Maybe you convinced him." The words are out before I remember who I'm talking to.

"What's that supposed to mean?"

I might as well back myself up. "I mean, maybe he finally saw you for who you are. Maybe he got fed up with your games."

"Oh, that's just perfect. I'm standing here, trying to get some answers. Trying to make sense of what's going on. And all you want to do is insult me." Her eyes grow wider as she talks and well up with tears.

And leave it to me to feel bad. After everything she's done to me, I suggest the plausible truth, and *I'm* the bad person. "Listen, Kennedy. I'm sorry. I just—"

"No. Own your words. You think you know me so well, is that it? You date my brother for a week, and suddenly you're the expert on the whole family? You're nothing but a liar. And a fake. And eventually, Miles will figure it out. You know what? I don't care if you talked to Devon—convinced him he should steer clear of me. You both can go to hell."

She turns away and starts down the sidewalk, walking away from the bar. A tiny part of me thinks I should follow her, but Kennedy can take care of herself. Shaking and pissed off, I go back into the bar just in time to see Red Head leaning close into Miles's ear. She whispers something and leans back, laughing, as though it was the best joke. Miles humors her with a half smile. I'm over it. If she's such a fan of the band, she can talk to the single guys. Try to lure *them* in. But it's time for her to get the hell away from my boyfriend.

I walk straight up to her, my head high. "I think you've spent enough time with Miles, and it's time for you to go."

She laughs, looking at Miles for his reaction and then back at me. Miles has on his best poker face as he drinks his beer.

"Do you have a problem with me?" she asks.

Again, here I go spitting out the truth. "You know? I do. You're a little too aggressive in the groupie department. And if you had any class, you wouldn't be trying to impede on someone else's relationship."

"Class? And what? You have it?" She stands up, letting the crazy side of her come out. "You think you can come up to me and tell me what to do?"

She reaches out and shoves me, pushing me into the people standing behind me, watching. Great. This is escalating quickly.

"Keep your hands off me," I tell her, my face serious. "If I were you, I'd walk away. Now."

"Well, I'm not you. And I'll do what I want."

She shoves me again, and this time I lose it. I pull my arm back, clench my fist, and swing with all my force, connecting with her jaw. She topples back onto the ground, and no one offers her help. I stand over her as she scrambles to get up. Then it turns into an all out catfight. She grasps for my hair, trying to fight the juvenile way, but the second she gets a handful and starts pulling, I hit her again, pushing her away. Everything's a whirl as we flail at each other, ready to stake our claim to what we think is rightfully ours. She thinks she can move in on Miles? She's crazy. Miles is mine, and I'll fight anyone for him. Her. Kennedy. Any other bitch who thinks they can control me.

Suddenly, hands are on me, pulling me away. I turn and see Miles holding tight to me. "Okay, killer. That's enough," he says.

A bouncer grabs Miley and directs her out the door while Miles leads me toward the back hallway. He pushes me into an office and closes the door behind us.

He gives me a once over, a slight smile playing at his lips. "What the hell was that?"

* * *

Miles

I don't know whether to think my girlfriend is insane or a badass. Where did this side of her come from?

"I ran into her this morning. She was pushy and fanatical about you."

"So she likes Tempest?" I don't get it. There are fans everywhere.

"No. Not just Tempest. *You.* I got a bad vibe from her this morning, and it only got worse tonight when she showed up again. Sorry. I shouldn't have gotten into a fight with her, but I wasn't going to let her—"

Like the strongest magnet, my mouth crushes into hers. I have to have her. That sort of intensity, that passion, it's so fucking hot. I kiss her hard, and pull away, her eyes dark as she looks up at me.

"What was that for?" she asks, breathless.

"For being the sexiest woman I know. No more fights. But that scene out there. You protecting your territory. Damn."

"You're not *territory*. You're—"

"Stop while you're ahead." I kiss her again, this time my hands gripping at her hips and running up her body. I cup her breasts as I kiss her, and I hear her moan softly. Her arms find their way around my neck, her fingers claw into my hair. She pulls herself closer to me, but I push her up against the wall.

Kissing her neck, I subtly reach over and lock the office door. Then my hands find the button to her cute jean shorts, and I unfasten them, unzip them, push them off her hips and hear them fall to the floor.

"What do you think you're doing?" she asks, quietly, playfully. She breathes in excited gasps and watches as I kneel down on my knees, lift her shirt, and kiss her belly.

I kiss her lower, trailing my tongue from her belly button to the elastic of the pink lacy panties she's wearing. I'm dying to taste her, to please her, to reward her for her act of courage out there.

Over her panties, I kiss the soft mound of flesh at the apex of her thighs. I hear her giggle and look up to find her looking around, worried, like she's scared we'll get caught.

"If you don't want to..." I tease her.

Abby looks down at me, her eyes filled with lust. Freeing one foot from her discarded shorts, she lifts her leg and wraps it around my shoulder, using it to pull me closer to her sex. Now I'm the one groaning with satisfaction at my up-close-and-personal view of one of the sexiest parts of her. Covered in the thin fabric of her panties is only more alluring and I lean in close, blindly kissing my way from her clit to the wet warmth I want to enter.

Every second, her panties grow wetter, and I use my fingers to tease the sensitive skin of her inner thighs. I'm taking my time, letting the fire build within her. My mouth only lingers for fleeting moments each time I kiss her, lick her. My fingers inch closer and closer to where I know she wants me to touch her. I've already learned she likes it fast and rough. I can only imagine what my slow, gentle touches must be doing to her.

Her leg around my shoulder starts trembling. Fingers yank at my hair trying to push my face into her. Her back arches away from the wall as she thrusts her hips forward. I guess that's my cue.

I force her back against the wall with my hands and then tug her panties to the side, exposing her to me. I smile as I go in for the ultimate kiss. My tongue plunges into her warmth while my thumb massages her clit in firm, slow circles. I hear Abby's hands slap against her mouth as she tries to contain her moans. Her muscles are already tightening as I taste her, so I kiss her harder and groan as I do. Abby lets out a scream, and as she lets herself come undone and comes for me, she tastes like bliss.

My mouth stays on her until she settles, and like a gentleman, I replace her panties and help her back into her shorts. See? It's like nothing ever happened.

Except the flush of Abby's skin, the sheen of sweat on both of us, the breathlessness of two people who bring each other more ecstasy than I ever could've imagined. I stand up and let her fall into me while she catches her breath. Holding her close, I whisper into her ear, "No woman will ever come between us. Is that clear?"

She wraps her arms around me, and looks up. "The only thing that's clear right now is how much disregard we have for somebody's workspace."

We both burst out laughing and sneak out of the office, more high than any drugs could make us. The whole night's been full of excitement—the show, Abby fighting for me, pleasing her in the office. Things couldn't possibly be better. And there's only one way to celebrate.

I stop by the bar and climb on top of it. The bartender below me looks equally curious and irritated, but everyone else is staring at me with anticipation, so I yell down to all of them.

"The next round is on me!"

*

Abby

I excuse myself to go to the bathroom, self-conscious and certain that I look like...well, that I look like Miles just ravaged me in somebody's office. When I come out of the women's restroom, I do a double-take. Okay, Atlanta is officially not my favorite city. First, Kennedy throws all her drama at me. Then, I get into a fight with Miley. And now, I'm looking across to the end of the bar to see none other than that Terrance guy from the coffee shop. But this one is on me, and I owe him an apology.

As I walk closer, I take him in. He looks like a normal guy, hanging out at a bar after a rock show. He's in a t-shirt and jeans, and there's still no sign of a camera. I highly doubt he's with *ScandalLust,* and since that was the worst of my concerns, it's obvious I overreacted this morning.

"Hi," I say, meekly.

He turns around and smiles warmly. "Well, hello, Ms. Clarke. It's nice to see you here."

"Yeah." I nod, now unsure what I should say. "Did you go to the show tonight?"

"I did. Pretty good. Then I noticed everyone was heading here." He holds up his beer. "A black IPA is the perfect end to the evening. Oh, did you want a drink? I can get you one—"

"Oh no. No thanks. I'm okay. Actually, I wanted to say sorry—about earlier? I was acting defensive, and I'm sure I came off really rude."

He waves his hand. "No apologies necessary. I shouldn't have surprised you the way I did. I caught you off guard."

"Either way, I'm not the kind of person to act so...unprofessionally. So my apologies."

"Then you're forgiven," he says with a wink, and I realize I don't want him to think I'm flirting with him either.

"Well, I need to get back over there." I motion my head toward Miles. "It was good seeing you again."

"You too, Ms. Clarke. Don't forget to try that diner while you're here."

I smile and hurry back to the comfort of Miles. At least now, my conscious is clear with Terrance. I hate drama and don't mind handing out an apology when it's due. That said, I don't think I'll *ever* find myself saying sorry to Miley. That crazy woman had it coming.

Miles wraps his arms around me and kisses my neck. All the while, an idea is forming in my head. If there's no drama, there's no story. How can we convince Polly Hemsworth—the head of *ScandalLust*—that Tempest is nothing but a boring, drama-free band?

I look Miles in the eye, suddenly excited. "I think I figured out our plan!"

Chapter Four

Abby

The next morning, Kennedy and I are standing face-to-face in my hotel room.

"I suggest you do what she says, Ken." Miles is sitting on the edge of the bed we slept in last night. "She can throw a mean right hook."

Kennedy lets out an exasperated sigh and points to my right hand. "That one."

I'm holding two of my own outfits in my arms, letting her decide which she'll be wearing to our *ScandalLust* interview. The one she picked includes a jean skirt and a flowery, white top.

"I don't have to wear your dumb boots, do I?" she asks.

I laugh at her. "I suggest that or sandals. Steer clear of heels. We want you looking sweet, not sexy." She rolls her eyes and snatches the clothes from me, stomping out of the room.

"So this is your grand plan? Turn Kennedy into you for the day?"

The thought makes me cringe. "Not exactly. And it's not just Kennedy getting a makeover. Now it's your turn."

Miles stands up fast, backing away from me. "Hell no. I'm fine the way I am."

"Oh I know you're fine. You're very sexy and mysterious and the bad boy I never knew I wanted." He's smiling big at the compliments. "But you can't be any of those things for this interview." His smile vanishes. "Now come here."

First, I give him a long kiss. Then I push him toward his suitcase. "Find the nicest shirt you've got in there. And a pair of jeans—but no holes in them." He finds the clothes quickly. "Good, now take a shower. Then I'll do your hair."

"Will you join me?"

It's tempting. "Not now, Romeo. I have to make sure your sister doesn't try to sneak out the fire escape."

A good forty-five minutes later, my work is complete. Minus the blue hair, Kennedy looks like she just walked off the streets of my hometown. I give her a side braid that cascades down one of her shoulders. Her makeup is subtle, giving her face a fresh, pure look. She looks sweet and innocent and is finally amused by our plan.

Looking in the mirror, she says to me, "You really think this will work?" One of her hands caresses her braid as she checks her silhouette. Normally, she's a fan of sexy corset tops and not-so-modest skirts. Maybe seeing herself looking...well, more like me will prove to her it's not so bad.

Meanwhile, Miles is walking back out of the bathroom. His usually disheveled hair is combed and smoothed into place. Matched with the button down and nice jeans, he looks more like a suave magazine model and less like a grungy rocker.

"If anyone sees me like this..." he says, clearly disapproving.

"They'll think you're gorgeous. Now get over yourself and lets get to this interview."

*

We arrive at a quiet restaurant, and I have to hold back a laugh as I watch Kennedy and Miles look cautiously over their shoulders.

"I don't see any paps." Miles thrusts his hands into his pockets and walks quickly inside.

"No paps means no cameras," Kennedy adds, and I can hear a hint of disappointment. She *wants* people to catch her in this charade.

Before leaving the hotel, I did another search for Polly Hemsworth and found enough photos to be able to spot her in a crowded room. I see her sitting at the bar, laughing with the bartender.

"You two wait out of sight. I want to make sure we really catch her off guard. We need the disappointment to be palpable."

Kennedy and Miles wander toward a hallway leading to the bathrooms while I approach Polly.

"Good afternoon, Ms. Hemsworth."

She spins on her stool, hops off, and eagerly shakes my hand. "Oh Abby. It's a pleasure to finally meet you in person."

I'm sure it is...

She continues, her voice chirpy and overly enthusiastic. "When you said you were ready to meet, I was so excited. I just knew you'd come through. To be honest, I've hardly slept. The suspense has been *killing* me."

I look around for the writer she'd said would be here. "Are we waiting for someone else to show up?"

Polly lets out a high-pitched laugh. "At the last minute I realized it. If I let someone else write this juicy story, then I don't get all the credit. So I sent Peter back to L.A. I'll be doing all the work myself. It'll be just us girls," she adds, playfully nudging my shoulder.

I've gotten used to Kennedy's fake kindness. Polly's act is on a whole different level. I do my best to match it.

"Well, let's get started then. Where would you like to sit?"

We find a quiet booth in one corner, and after a server stops by to take Polly's order— I'm too nervous to be hungry—she cuts right to the chase.

"So what do you have for me? I've been onto this band for some time now, but you know *ScandalLust*. We're notorious for posting our breaking news a second too early. I wanted more evidence to back me up this time. Nobody will be able to turn away."

"Great. I do have some proof for you. Actually, physical proof. Would you like to see it?"

"Of course!"

I stand up. "Give me just a second."

Polly's drumming her hands on her knees as I walk away. Her anticipation is plastered all over her face. It's a little sickening how excited she is, thinking she's about to break major news that would ruin people's lives.

As soon as I spot Miles and Kennedy, I wave them over. They follow me back to the booth, and I watch Polly closely, waiting for her reaction. She sees my physical proof, and her face flushes white. Just as quickly, all negative expression vanishes as a huge smile stretches across her lips.

The three of us slide into the booth across from Polly. Miles, myself, and Kennedy. It's a three-on-one attack Polly didn't see coming.

"Wow. Ms. Clarke. You've outdone your-self, but when we talked..." She nods her head toward Miles and Kennedy as though she's being subtle. "Well, I didn't think it was nec-essary to bring them into the mix. After all, they're very busy with their tour and...other activities." She's referring to the supposed drug and prostitution ring. It's unbelievable how this woman thinks it's actually true.

"When you asked for proof, it took awhile to find it. Then it dawned on me. My friends, Miles and Kennedy are all the proof you need. So we talked, and they agreed to let you have an exclusive interview with them. Ask them anything," I tell her, almost like it's a dare. "They're an open book."

* * *

Miles

I always said I hated the tabloids, and this Polly woman isn't making my opinion any better. She's been grilling me and Ken for the past half hour, while stuffing her face with cheese fries and a vanilla shake. Shit, when I first found out Abby was going on tour with us, I assumed she was one of them. The difference between the tabloid trash in front of me and my girlfriend beside me couldn't be more obvious.

"So in the past year, how many sexual partners have you had, Kennedy? And how many of them have had to pay you to receive your...services."

Kennedy sits up taller, and I nearly laugh. It's a good thing she's not planning on answering honestly anyway. "That's a deeply personal question, Ms. Hemsworth," Kennedy says in her most proper voice, "but in honor of being truthful, I'll tell you. I've been with one man. My faithful, loving boyfriend, Devon Stone. That shouldn't be much of a surprise to you. After all, Devon and I have been very public about our affection toward each other."

Never mind all the other people they've been affectionate toward. But who am I to talk? I had my fair share of whoring around up until I met Abby. I still don't get how she changed that part of me so suddenly...

"But Kennedy, there are sources who say you've traded sexual acts for other things, such as money, clothes, jewelry—"

"No ma'am. That's not true at all. I would never cheat on Devon."

Polly lets out a huff. She's gotten nowhere with this interview. Next, she turns back to me.

"All right, then, Miles. Tell me about other activities you've engaged in, either with the band or on your own."

"I'm sorry. I don't understand. What do you mean by *engaged?*"

Of course, I know what she wants me to say, but it's way more fun to frustrate the hell out of her.

"Illegal activities, Miles. What have you been involved in? Does the band know or have you kept it behind their backs?"

"Illegal activities... Like what, Ms. Hemsworth? I can't think of anything—"

"Drug trafficking, production, other illegal business activities... Any of that ring a bell?"

I pretend to think for a really long time. Long enough, that even Kennedy is growing impatient waiting for me to speak. I reach across the table and steal one of Polly's fries. Eating it slowly, I let a grin form on my face. "You know...there was this one time. We were back home in L.A., and this drug dealer asked me if I wanted to buy anything from him. But I said no. I'm really not into that scene."

Polly stares at me, her fake friendliness long gone. "You really expect me to believe that? You two can come in here looking all prim and proper, but I've seen you. You aren't the angels you're pretending to be."

"I'm afraid the act is left on stage." I stretch my arm across the back of the booth, behind Abby, and rest my hand on Kennedy's shoulder. "We're just your average people when the show's over. I know that must be a disappointment for you, but whomever convinced you we were anything other than law abiding citizens was wrong. You're welcome to come tour with us like Abby's done. You'll see we're much more into video games and sleeping in than drugs and sexual deviance." I think back to the strippers and threesomes. The lies spewing from my mouth are golden. "Any other questions?"

*

Polly's red in the face by the time she says goodbye and stomps away. Once she's out of sight, the three of us turn to each other unable to contain our laughter anymore.

"I can't believe that worked," Kennedy says, scoping out the basket of fries to see if there are any left.

I kiss the top of Abby's head. "You're a genius."

"I wouldn't go that far. Now we wait and see. If they keep following you guys around and publishing their bullshit stories, then we'll have to think of a Phase 2. But...judging by her disappointment, I'm pretty sure she's over you. It's a waste of time and money to keep chasing a story with no leads."

"Well, I'll give this one to you." Kennedy raises her hand and high fives Abby. "You're better at this game than I gave you credit for."

Call me surprised. Is Kennedy genuinely being nice to Abby? Maybe we'll see a change of attitude from her. Maybe... But probably not.

"Now let's get back to the hotel so I can get out of this god forsaken outfit." Kennedy's up and walking toward the doors before Abby can finish rolling her eyes.

We leave with our heads high, feeling good about our small victory. To think, I didn't even have to punch somebody to make my point. I could get used to this.

Outside, the Atlanta sun is scorching. We make a quick right to head back to the hotel, but we're not five feet down the sidewalk when we stop short. A lump forms in my throat and my fists automatically clench.

When we first booked Atlanta on this trip, my instincts said this was a bad idea. Too much history. Too much risk. And this is precisely why.

Walking toward me, eyes glued to mine, is a man I'd spot anywhere. He keeps his hair shorter these days, looking more like a businessman than the rock star wannabe he was while he ran Graffiti Rock Records.

Stopping in front of me, it's obvious this run-in was no coincidence. I set my jaw firm, waiting to hear what he has to say. This is the guy who had me sent to jail. He's the reason I had to recreate myself. He's the source of all my baggage—why I have to play it safe, why I have to keep the peace, why I have to protect my secrets.

"Miles," he says, a smug grin on his face. He looks over at Abby, giving her a once over and a wink, and I could fight him again right here for looking at my girlfriend like that. "I like the name change. It suits you."

I shake my head slowly. "Terrance. What the hell do you want?"

Chapter Five

Abby

I immediately feel like the biggest fool. Terrance *does* know Miles, and judging by the tension between the two of them, it's obvious he's not the nice guy he claimed to be.

"What's going on, Miles?" I ask him quietly.

Miles doesn't look my way, and at first I don't think he's even heard me. But then he takes a step closer to Terrance. "Nothing's going on. He was just leaving, weren't you?"

Terrance stares him down, unrelenting, and I feel the adrenaline start pulsing through me. We did so well, dealing with *ScandalLust* without any violence. Would Miles really screw it all up in a matter of minutes after convincing Polly there wasn't a story worth following?

"Miles here is just an old friend," Terrance says, a smug grin on his face. "We've got a long history, but there's no need to dwell in the past, right buddy?"

Miles doesn't say a word. I can't begin to imagine what he's thinking, but his body's taut and his glare is fiery. There's no way these two were ever friends.

Terrance finally takes a step back and laughs. "Relax. You're on tour, after all. So close to hitting it big." He lowers his voice. "And I sincerely hope you get everything you deserve."

With that, he passes between us and walks away. I turn and watch him go, completely confused. That conversation answered none of my questions. I turn back to Miles, but he's several feet ahead of me walking back to the hotel. I pick up my pace to catch up.

"Can you explain that one to me? That Terrance guy, he—" I start to tell him I talked to him already, but Miles cuts in.

"That's the asshole who ran Graffiti Rock."

Oh. Wow. "The one you got in the fight with?"

"The one who pressed charges and got me in this situation? Yeah. That's him."

We reach the hotel and head toward its double doors. I'm tempted to point out that Miles got himself into that whole situation, but I bite my tongue. He's dealing with the consequences, and this whole new revelation about Terrance is far more important. Again, I open my mouth to tell him Terrance found me first, but as soon as we're in the lobby, Eddie comes out of nowhere and pins his hand against Miles's chest, stopping him in his tracks.

"We need to have a little discussion," Eddie says, his voice filled with fury. He looks over at me. "I'm borrowing your boyfriend." He then pushes Miles back toward the doors, and they're both gone before I can get a word in.

What was *that* about? I quickly try to piece everything I know together. Eddie is Miles's probation officer and band manager. He's definitely the one who calls the shots, which Miles very clearly hates. So what did he do to piss off Eddie? Does Eddie know Terrance is here? Maybe he approached him too...

I go up to our suite and close myself into my room, collapsing on the bed. My mind's working overtime right now, trying to make sense of everything. What did Terrance want with me? Oh god, did I say anything I shouldn't have? Am I the one who gave up Miles's identity?

No, he already knew. That's got to be how he recognized me. But what was he trying to accomplish by meeting with me? Why not go straight to the source? He knew where Miles was this whole time. The whole thing makes me sick to my stomach. Something's going on, and I hate not knowing what it is.

I cover my face with my hands and take a deep breath, trying to relax. Letting out a frustrated huff, I sit up on the edge of the bed and spot the pretty blue acoustic guitar sitting in the corner. Well, there's one way to make my hurried mind chill out. I grab the guitar and sit back down. The feel of it in my arms is comforting and familiar. My acoustic at my apartment gets a lot of use from me, especially when I'm approaching deadlines and feeling stressed. The first strum of this one, and I'm amazed. Don't get me wrong. I love my guitar. I've had it for years, but this one. This one sounds like gold.

I'm not much of a songwriter, but I've written a few things over time. Starting on one of the songs, I close my eyes and listen to each chord—each note—as I start singing.

It's a stupid song, nothing that would ever end up on the radio, but it's all about my childhood. Summer days, sibling fights, bonding with my dad. There's something about playing this particular song that eases all my troubles, and it's helping now, even though the troubles I'm dealing with aren't even my own. They're Miles's. I wish I could calm him the same way.

When I feel a weight shift on the bed behind me, I nearly jump out of my skin. I never heard the door open, but when I spin around, Miles is there, sitting behind me, a sexy smile on his face.

"Don't stop. I want to hear you play more."

My cheeks flush with warmth. No way. I'm not a performer. Not like him. "Maybe some other time." I let out a nervous laugh, feeling a little embarrassed that he heard any of that. But then I remember all the troubles I was trying to sing away. "What did Eddie want?"

Miles lies back in the bed, stretching his long legs past me. I watch his chest rise and fall with his steady breaths. How can he be so relaxed?

"He was pissed we met with *ScandalLust*."

It never crossed my mind that we should've included Eddie in our charade. Of course, it would've been the right thing to do, to run it past him.

Miles takes my hand. "It's fine," he says with a laugh. "I told him what we did, and he was actually a little impressed. Why are you so stressed?"

Why am I? How can he *not* be? "I think we should talk about this Terrance situation."

He shakes his head no, grabs the guitar out of my lap, and sets it on the floor. The next thing I know, I'm lying down on the bed, and Miles is hovering over me. I run my hands through his nice, neat hair, messing up this morning's work. He leans in and kisses me, his tongue dancing with mine. A calming warmth floods through me, and I forget what we needed to talk about as I kiss him back.

"You have a sexy singing voice," he tells me when he pulls away from my lips.

"Thanks, but I was singing about a lemonade stand."

"I don't care what you were singing about." Miles drops a kiss on my forehead and another on my cheek. "I want to hear you sing more."

"You can quit Tempest and we'll start a band together." I'm clutching his shirt in my hands as I joke about having a future in music.

He continues the ridiculous fantasy. "We'd go on tour, just the two of us on the bus, with all the time in the world." He kisses my neck and my breath catches. "Then we'd play shows, and each one would end with a private after party—just you, me, and unlimited opportunities to make you come for me." He drops his body onto mine, and the weight of him makes my whole body scream for more. I need him closer to me.

Heat flashes through me again. "We'd be the most unproductive band. I doubt we'd ever make it out onto the stage." I unbutton his shirt and rip at it until it tugs away. My hands trace the lines along his chest and run down his tight, muscled back. I pull my legs out from under him, and spread them around his waist.

He pushes himself against me harder, and I hate every inch of fabric that still separates us. "You're right about that," he says in a low growl. Then he yanks my shirt over my head and his mouth explores all the exposed skin of my breasts.

I arch my back to encourage him. In a flurry of fumbling and tugging, we rid each other of the rest of our clothes, throwing them off the bed into a tangled pile on the floor. Breathless, I stare up into Miles's dark eyes. I love the way he's looking at me. It's like he has nothing to hide, and the way he feels about me seems to be written across his face, a mix of gentle adoration and intense lust. I want to hold onto him forever.

Lifting my head, I lure Miles closer with a kiss. His lips crush into mine and he rolls us over, putting me on top of him. His hands run down my back, cupping my bare ass, and pressing me against his growing hardness. I let out a moan and sit up, rolling my hips against him and savoring the look of pleasure that crosses his face.

Miles reaches across the bed, opening the side table next to us, and pulls out a condom. I take it from him, doing the honors, and as soon as he's ready for me, I know I'm ready for him.

I position myself over him and slide him into me, slowly, taking in every inch. I start riding him, and my head falls back, my eyes close, from how good he feels.

Miles grips my hips as I move. I look down at him, not feeling even slightly self-conscious as he watches me. I'm amazed by how I find him sexier every time I see him naked. His tan skin is taut against his tight chest and defined abs. Tattoos wrap around his nipples and across his stomach—intricate black lines, a grim reaper, and the word "fearless". If I could reach, I'd kiss my way along those lines, but I settle for trailing my fingers along them, tracing the ink. This is definitely the most gorgeous man I've ever had sex with.

"You're so beautiful," he says to me, as if reciprocating my thoughts. And I feel it too.

He makes me feel invincible, limitless—like I can be anyone I want to be when I'm with him. I nearly laugh remembering how superficial I thought he was when we first met. Hell, he was. But something shifted after our first kiss. Something's been growing ever since, and whatever we have, it's something that could really last.

Now we're here, two bodies as one. He pulls me down on top of him, rolling over onto me, and kissing me hard. He thrusts himself deeper into me, and I'm filled with ecstasy.

His lips find my ear and he kisses my earlobe before whispering, "No one makes me feel the way you do."

I claw my fingers into his back as he takes me faster. His body, starting to sweat, is hot and rigid as we undulate in a quickening rhythm. I hold on to him with my legs, letting him full access to slam into my sex. Inside, the pressure rises fast. His mouth on mine takes my breath away as I try to breathe and kiss and feel every second of this moment at the same time. His teeth close on my bottom lip, tugging lightly, and in his next thrust, I feel my entire body come undone—a tidal wave of ecstasy rushing through me. Moans escape me, and I tremble with his every touch. He buries his face in my neck and growls along with his own release. The grunts turn to gasps as he empties himself into me. He rolls off me and we lay side-by-side, the rest of the world spinning, as we try to settle our thundering hearts.

Giddy like a schoolgirl, I immerse myself in the happiness he brings me. I hear Miles take a long, deep breath and then reach down, picking up his guitar. He rests it on his chest as he thoughtlessly strums a few notes. Let me just say, this picture perfect image— Miles, naked, a beautiful guitar positioned across him—is camera worthy. I'd even let *ScandalLust* in the room if it meant saving this image forever.

I turn onto my side, propping myself up on my elbow as I watch him play. He looks at me and gives me a sly wink before switching to a song I do recognize.

"She leaves me breathless
Mind a blur"

My heart swells, and I sing the next line with him.

"Fate's dirty tricks"

"See? We sound good together," he says with a smirk. He sings one last line, changing his original lyrics, "*Now I've got her.*" Then he pushes the guitar toward me. "Here."

"I'm not in any shape to play right now." I hold up my right hand to show it's still shaking, the aftershocks of a great orgasm.

"You don't have to. I want you to have this."

"The guitar?"

"No, just one of the strings." He laughs. "Yes, the guitar. It's yours. Far more your style than mine anyway."

"You don't have to do that." He's still holding it out for me to take, so I grab it, and sit up, hugging it against me.

"Yeah I do. I want you to keep playing. I want you to write more. And if you don't, you'll make me feel bad, and I know you don't want to do that."

I smile. So he's *guilting* me into playing music. "And how will you serenade me without it?"

"You mean distortion pedals and double bass don't make your heart swoon?" He doesn't wait for me to answer. "I'm sure you'll let me borrow it, or, better yet, I'll just take it as I please when I'm at your place."

The thought of Miles in my apartment is both bizarre and perfect. I wonder what Chord will think of him. "Well, thank you." I run my hand along the side of the guitar. It's the nicest thing anyone has ever given me, that's for sure. I set it next to me, and lean down to kiss him again. "Thank you," I repeat.

We lay together in bed for a while before remembering the real world is out there waiting for us.

"We're going to that bar again tonight. Want to get dressed and head over?" he asks.

I nod, and an unwelcome image flashes in my mind. Last night's run-in with Terrance at that bar. Would he be there again?

"There's something I need to tell you first."

Miles stands up and rummages through our clothes, finding his boxers.

I don't know where to start, so I blurt it all out. "Terrance approached me at a coffee shop yesterday morning. Didn't say who he was, but he wanted to know about you—"

"What did you tell him?" His voice is dead serious now. He tugs his jeans back on, glaring at me, waiting for an answer.

"Nothing." I quickly say. "Nothing. I thought he could be from the tabloids or something. I wasn't going to tell someone I don't know any information about you. But he gave me his card and left. I even felt bad, he was so polite about it. Then I ran into him at the bar last night—"

"He was there?" He shakes his head in disapproval. "That asshole."

"I talked to him. He was nice. I had no idea he was...*that* guy. If I'd known I would've told you right away."

"But you didn't. You should've told me as soon as you realized it."

"I tried. But you were pissed, and then Eddie took you, and then..." I let my words trail off so he could fill in the blanks. *And then we were in here having sex.* "I couldn't find the right time. I'm sorry."

"It's fine," he says bluntly. He yanks a t-shirt from his bag and pulls it over his head. "You said he gave you a card?"

I nod and get out of bed, wrapping the sheet around my naked body. I find the card in my purse and hand it to him. "It doesn't have much on it. That's why I didn't know who he really was."

He stares at the card for a second before jamming it into his pocket along with his cell phone and steps into his shoes. "It's got enough."

And without another word, he leaves the room, letting the door slam behind him.

"Miles!" I yell after him in a panic. I'm in no state to follow him. As fast as I can, I get back into my own clothes. I throw my hair in-to a messy ponytail on top of my head, slide into a pair of sandals, and run out the door after him. But by the time I get to the lobby and out the front doors, it's too late. He's gone.

Oh no, Miles. What are you going to do?

Chapter Six

Miles

"You get into another fight with your girl?" Nate asks me, a smug tone in his voice. The asshole followed me out of the hotel, and I don't have time to tell him to fuck off.

Ignoring him, I pull out my phone and Terrance's card and call the number printed on it. It goes to voicemail.

"Listen carefully, you bastard. It's one thing to track me down. But to go after my girlfriend first? You've crossed a line. I'll be seeing you very soon." I hang up, and hear Nate behind me again.

"Hey, man. What's going on?"

"Not right now, Nate. Go back to the hotel."

He quickens his pace so he's right next to me. "Not until you tell me what's going on. Something happen?" When I continue to avoid his questions, he steps directly in front of me, planting his hands on my chest.

I shove him, but he doesn't get the hint.

"Go the fuck away, Nate."

"What the hell is wrong with you? Something's going on, and you're going to tell me what it is. Damn. I can help you, man. Let me help."

"You want to help?" He doesn't know the first thing about Terrance, the old label, my history. What the hell can he do to help? "You can help by getting your hands off of me."

He relents and we start walking again. "Where are we going?"

I look down at the card. The address on it is downtown, probably close to the coffee shop Abby went to, which explains how he's been tracking her so easily. "Not far," is all I tell Nate.

"And what are we doing?"

"Revisiting my past."

I can see from the corner of my eye that he's clueless, confused. "Care to elaborate?"

I shake my head. "If you really want to help, make sure I don't do anything really stupid." I look over at him to show I'm serious. "Keep me out of jail."

*

We walk the rest of the way in silence, and when we get to the address, I see it's a used record store. Is this what Terrance is doing now? The door makes a clinging sound as I pull it open. Nate and I look around. Records line the walls in bins, a few instruments hang above them, and in the back, it looks like there's a small recording studio.

The only person I see is some high school-aged kid behind a counter.

"Terrance here?"

He looks at me and his eyes go wide. "Are you? You're Miles Riot. Dude, I saw—"

"Terrance," I say again. "Is he here?"

"In the back."

I start walking while the kid tells me he liked last night's show. Nate's still acting like a confused, loyal dog, staying at my side. As soon as we're near the back of the store, I spot an open door leading into a messy office. I burst through the doorway, and find Terrance sitting at a desk.

"What the fuck do you want from me?"

He jumps out of his chair, and for a second, I savor the surprise and fear that flashes across his face. But he erases it quickly, and returns to his tough guy, cocky grin.

"Nice to see you too."

"You're going to leave me alone. You're going to leave my girlfriend alone. And—"

"And what, Matthew? Sorry—*Miles*. What will happen if I don't? Because the last time I checked, you don't have very many options that'll end well for you."

To hell with him and my probation. I step forward, ready to get in his face, but two hands grab me from behind and pull me back out of the office.

"Let go of me, Nate!"

"I may not have a clue what the hell this is about, but you're not fighting this guy."

I whirl around, glaring at Nate. Then I push past him and punch the wall behind him. Terrance follows us out of the office.

"You know, Miles? I don't think I will be leaving you alone. See? We started something a long time ago that I'd like to finish. Call it fate. Or maybe karma. But now that we've been reunited, I'm going to see to it that you get a taste of your own medicine. I'm going to watch you suffer."

He's taunting me, and my body buzzes with adrenaline. I could smash his face in. Nate looks from Terrance to me and back to Terrance.

"What the hell are you talking about?" he asks him.

"I thought you bands were like family..." He's still looking at me while he answers Nate. "I guess Miles didn't tell you how he screwed me over. How he tore down my career and walked away laughing. Oh wait, he didn't exactly walk away."

"Just drop it, Terrance. How do I get you to leave me alone?"

He laughs. "It's not that simple. You aren't going to pay me off. I'm not going anywhere."

"You're a real prick, aren't you?" Nate's standing between us and inches closer. "He asked what you want. How about you man up and let go of this little grudge you're holding?"

Nate's trying to keep the peace. It's noble of him, but Terrance isn't the type who thinks rationally.

"Let me guess. You're used to playing the wingman for fuckboy here, right? The reliable sidekick to the man in the spotlight? You know? If you'd grow a pair and ask the right questions, you might find out who your boyfriend really is."

In a flash, Nate's fist slams into Terrance's jaw. "You have no idea who I am," he says in a threatening voice, shoving Terrance back and clenching his fist harder, ready to hit him again.

In seconds, the two are on the ground, fists flying. Nate tackles Terrance beneath him, and the sound of his knuckles colliding with the flesh of Terrance's face makes me cringe. My body jolts, ready to jump in and help pummel him, but I stop myself. I can't fight him. I can't screw up my probation. And as much as I want to let Nate beat the shit out of him, we need to get the hell out of here before there's a bigger problem.

I pull Nate away. "He's not worth it. Let's go."

Nate stares Terrance down as I push him to the front of the store. I back into the door, pushing it open, and yank Nate out with me, only to find we have more company.

"Shit."

To our left, the street's blocked by two SUVs. A half dozen paparazzi are armed and ready with their cameras pointed our way. The flickering lights from their flashes compete with the strobing lights to our right where three cop cars wait.

I pinch the bridge of my nose and let out a frustrated sigh. The asshole must have tipped them off the second Nate and I walked into the store. And I'll bet a thousand dollars the smug jerk is standing behind me right now with a grin on his face.

I turn around. Yep. I'd like to punch his teeth in, but not with this street party watching.

"Officer, this is the guy," Terrance says, pushing past me while pointing at me at the same time. "He's the one who did this." He shows the cop his bloodied mouth.

"He's lying," I shout behind him. "I didn't touch him."

"Listen, sir." Terrance moves in closer to the cop like they're old buds. They speak quietly and I can barely make out what he's telling him. "...has a history of issues...run his record...Matthew Smith, but he goes by Miles Riot these days."

The cop looks at Terrance like he's an annoying bug. I don't blame him. I wish I could squash him under my shoe. All the while, the cameras are going crazy as the paps try to get in closer. Another officer pushes them back, telling them to give us space or they'll all be arrested.

I'm trying like hell to keep my cool. Terrance is up to something. It's like he had all this planned even though Nate and I showed up unannounced. Speaking of Nate...

"What the hell is he doing? You didn't hit him." He's standing next to me, his arms tightly crossed.

The officer leaves Terrance and walks up to me. I'm hoping he's not buying Terrance's bullshit. He's got to see this guy's a weasel.

"Let's see some ID."

Nate and I both reach into our pockets to retrieve our wallets, but the officer stops Nate. "Not you. You can go."

"I'm the one who was involved in the fight. Why wouldn't you want to see mine?"

The officer rolls his eyes. "Sure. You guys want to be a team, so be it." He holds his hand out, and we each slap our driver's license into his palm. He walks away without a word, returning to his car.

I glare at Terrance. He sees me for a second but averts his eyes quickly. That damn grin is still on his face. The next thing I know, the officer is getting statements from Terrance, then from Terrance's jackass employee inside the store—he's obviously the one who called them. And then he comes back to me and Nate.

"Come with me," he tells Nate, and they walk back into the store.

Now all I can do is wait, and I'm growing more pissed by the second. I shouldn't have come here. I should've known better. Too late. Shit's going to hit the fan, and there's no getting out of it.

When Nate comes back out, the officer inside calls to me, "Your turn, rock star."

I shove my hands into my pockets and walk in. I'm just going to tell him the truth. He's got to believe me.

"I've got two witnesses saying you came here and assaulted Mr. Young. Then your buddy swears he did everything. So what do you have to say?"

"I came here to talk to him. He went after my girlfriend, and I was coming by to tell him to back the f—to back off. I'm on tour. I'll be out of Atlanta tomorrow. He just needed to leave us alone until then."

"And since he wasn't leaving you alone, you felt the need to smash in his face?"

"I told you, that wasn't me."

"Let me see your hands."

I hold them up. He turns them over to look at the knuckles. Dammit. I punched the fucking wall. My right hand shows it.

"So you didn't hit him..." He doesn't believe a word I'm saying.

"Nate hit him. He shouldn't have. He was defending me, that's all."

"Or maybe he's defending you now, because he knows what's going to happen to you."

He means my ass will get tossed in jail. "He doesn't even know about all that."

The officer nods his head, a condescending expression on his face. He's not buying it. "So tell me about the phone call."

"The what—"

"Don't play dumb. Mr. Young just shared a voicemail from you, from approximately ten minutes before you attacked him. Want to explain that?"

"I was pissed. They were just words. I didn't touch him. I said—"

"You've said enough. Two witnesses say it was you, your buddy is trying to take the fall, and your record tells me this wasn't an isolated incident. So you know what I need you to do next."

My stomach sinks as I turn my back on the officer and place my hands behind me. Seconds later, I feel the cold steel of cuffs. He starts reading me my rights as he pats me down, looking for anything I shouldn't have on me. Sorry man. No gun. No drugs. Nothing. *I'm innocent*, I want to scream at him, but the sea of flashes outside tells me now's not the time to lose it. It's all being recorded and will be on the front page of *ScandalLust* by morning. So much for getting them off my tail.

As he leads me outside and into the back of the police car, only one thought sticks in my mind.

I'm sorry, Abby.

Chapter Seven

Abby

I'm a nervous wreck waiting for Miles to get back. It's been over two hours. I wish I'd memorized all the information on Terrance's business card. It's obvious he went to the address that was on there. But all I can do is wait, pacing our room. The rest of the suite is quiet. Last I saw, Dax was on the couch, getting high and staring blankly at the TV.

Kennedy and Nate are nowhere to be seen, and all the groupies have cleared out.

It's lonely. And quiet. The thumping of my worried heart is thunderous in the silence.

Then I hear the beep of the door being unlocked, and I rush out of the room. Thank god he's back. I'll calm him down. Convince him everything will be okay, and we'll get out of Atlanta as soon as possible.

My hope is deflated when I see it's just Eddie and Nate. I turn to go back in the room to wait some more, but I hear Eddie behind me. "Abby, we need to talk."

Dread floods through me. The only thing he and I have in common is Miles. If he needs to talk to me, then... I turn and see the look in his eyes—anger, disappointment, worry. What happened?

I walk to the edge of the couch and sit on its arm, waiting to hear what Eddie has to say.

Instead of talking, he turns to Nate. "Why don't you tell her what you two nimrods did?"

Nate looks at me and gulps. "I followed Miles to that guy's store—Terrance, I guess his name is. I didn't know anything was going to happen, I swear, but the asshole started shit with Miles. Miles had asked me to keep him out of trouble, so I handled it. I punched the guy. We got in a fight. The cops showed up. And the fuckers wouldn't believe me. Terrance told them it was all Miles, while I admitted it was me. Fuck them." He turns and paces between the living area and kitchen. When he turns back around, he runs his hands over the sides of his head, narrowly missing his mohawk. "They arrested him, Abby."

The rock in my stomach transforms into a boulder in a split second. I shake my head. "No. No—tell me that's not true."

"I'm sorry. I did everything I could."

"Along with starting the fight," Eddie throws in. He's visibly pissed off—heavy breathing, hands wringing, if his hair wasn't already flecked with gray, I would've believed this incident caused it.

I can't keep my thoughts straight. I have so many questions. Where did they take Miles? What are they going to do to him? How did he let this happen? What's it mean for the band? The tour? Where can I find Terrance so I can beat the crap out of him myself?

Eddie fills in the rest of the details, about how the cops and paparazzi all showed up. How they ran a check on Miles's history, which aligned to everything Terrance said, even if he did lie about the fight itself. Then there was some incriminating voicemail Miles left Terrance right before. Oh, I could strangle Miles for that one.

My thoughts are about to get the best of me when they're interrupted by a completely unexpected noise. Laughter. I look to my right where Dax is still lounging on the couch. He's still staring off into space, high as a kite, but now he's laughing like he's watching the funniest thing on TV. I glance at the

TV to see there's an infomercial playing...
Definitely not the source of his amusement.

"Are you finding this funny?"

He slowly looks over at me, a goofy smile
still slathered across his face. "What? You
don't?"

"Not even a little," I tell him. "My boyfriend is in jail. *Your* guitarist and half your
vocals is in jail. You remember you're in the
middle of a tour, right? So tell me what part
of that is funny."

Dax glances over at Eddie and Nate and
then shrugs his shoulders. "Guess you had to
be there," he says as though he'd witnessed
the apparently comedic arrest himself.

I could scream. Not necessarily at Dax—
it's useless arguing with someone who's
high—but at the whole situation in general.
How could this happen?

The door beeps again, and my heart leaps
for a second, forgetting where Miles is. No
way can it be him, which only leaves one other
person...Kennedy.

I'd rate my reaction to Miles being arrested as pretty rational. I'm controlling my urge to lash out. My hands are only a little shaky. No one can tell how upset I am from the outside. Kennedy, on the other hand... I already knew she was dramatic, but as Eddie tells her about Miles, she goes from one end of the coping spectrum to the other.

"This is a joke, right?" She lets out a little laugh and then looks around the room as if Miles is going to jump out any second.

"It's not a joke, Ken," Nate says quietly.

Her smile slowly fades as reality kicks in. Next thing I know, she's a crumpled pile on the floor. We wait in silence as she sits there, her face in her hands, her shoulders trembling every few seconds. The lack of noise is frightening.

Finally, she sits up, staring blankly ahead of her. "Tell me what happened."

This time, Nate relays all the details. It's just as painful to hear it again. *Where are you, Miles?* Is he still in a police car somewhere? Is he locked behind bars? It breaks my heart that I can't go and be with him right now.

Kennedy takes in all this new information, before subtly nodding her head. She slowly pulls herself back up to standing, takes a couple haphazard steps to her right, does an about face, and walks toward me.

The palm of her hand flies across my face. I feel the stinging sensation before I register the fact she just hit me.

"What the hell?" I shout, standing up and pushing her away from me.

"This is all your fault," she says, and then she stomps out of the suite.

Like hell is she going to slap me like that, accuse me of making this happen, and then walk away. My face still stinging, tears threaten to spill out of my eyes, but I refuse to let her have that effect on me. Screw the pain. I rush out of the suite, catch up to her in the hallway, and grab her shoulder, slamming her into the wall next to us.

"How can you think I had anything to do with this?"

"Are you kidding? Talking to the tabloids, getting involved with my brother, putting the spotlight all over him...Why else do you think it was so easy for Terrance to track him down?" She slides down the wall, sitting down, and runs her hands through her hair.

"The tabloids were already after you guys. The record labels and fame are what put you all in the spotlight, and your brother is a grown man. Did you ever stop to think he actually cares about me? That we care about each other? Your tantrums may have worked in the past, but I'm not going anywhere, and right now, we have bigger things to figure out." Feeling awkward about standing over Kennedy, I step back and sit against the opposite wall, facing her.

She shakes her head. "I can't believe this is happening. And right now. It couldn't be worse timing."

"I know. The tour and—"

"Not the tour. The last thing I want to do is get on a stage right now." She doesn't look up to see me scrunch my forehead. *Kennedy* doesn't want to be performing? I find that hard to believe. But then she continues. "Devon broke up with me. For real this time."

"It wasn't *for real* all the other times?"

She throws a glare at me. "No. Everything before was just...bullshit. But he's done with me. Says from now on, our relationship is strictly professional, if that."

I have few reasons to care about Kennedy's feelings, but I can see the hurt on her face. She lost her boyfriend and her brother the same day, and there's no telling if or when she'll get either back. *Don't think like that.* We will get Miles back, that's for sure.

"You don't want to hear this right now, I know, but I promise there's a better guy out there for you. You shouldn't have to be in a relationship where everything is always so uncertain, where you're always fighting. You should be with someone who keeps you happy, who brings out the best in you. Devon doesn't seem to be that person."

Kennedy opens her mouth to object, but changes her mind. After a second, she says, "Dammit. I don't want you to be right."

I'm not sure if that means she doesn't want to take advice from me or that she doesn't want to believe Devon's not the one for her. Maybe both...

"So is that what you think you have with my brother?" she asks. Her tone is only slightly condescending this time.

"I think we have something good. I really do. But none of that matters right now. We have to get him out of jail."

An eternity of silence passes before either of us speaks again, the heaviness of the situation really weighing on us now.

"I don't have a plan," Kennedy says, meekly.

I can't help but look at her and smile. "Me neither." For once, we're on the same, unfortunate page.

We get up and return to the suite, hoping Eddie's got something figured out.

"The best case scenario," he says, "we get a quick court date and convince the judge this is all a big misunderstanding."

I'm having trouble with this concept of relying on another source of authority to take Miles's word about this. "And what if he doesn't believe him, just like the cop?"

Eddie looks at me, all expression gone. "We can't think like that. Let's just focus on getting back to L.A. so we can take care of this."

"Is that where—" I start but my voice breaks and betrays me.

"Yeah. They're flying him back to county tonight. Everything will be dealt with there with the same judge as last time. I'm meeting with everyone tomorrow at the L.A. offices."

I nod my head in understanding and walk toward my room, closing the door behind me. Taking a deep breath, I promise myself we'll get through this. Miles will be fine. Our relationship will be fine. Everything will be okay.

There's not much left to do but begin packing. Without Miles here, I take it upon myself to gather his things for him. I retrieve toothbrushes and hair products from the bathroom, shove them into our bags, and then start collecting clothes strewn all over the place. Miles is sort of a slob. I almost laugh—almost. But the odd sound catches in my throat. I gulp it back.

Lifting one of his black shirts from the arm of a chair, I bring it to my face, nuzzling it against my cheek. The soft fabric, the scent of Miles—musky cologne and a hint of sweat—and the whole room seems to crash down around me. I fall into the bed, still hugging Miles's shirt close to me. My eyes sting as the tears fall freely now.

How could this happen?

How do I save him?

Why, after all this time, would Terrance come after Miles? Come after me?

That's it. Terrance. He can't get away with this. And I can't leave Atlanta without getting answers.

At some point, I fall asleep crying, missing Miles. It's amazing how someone still so new to me can leave such a vast, empty space when he's not here. But I don't fall asleep a helpless, hopeless woman. I have a plan. Well, a start of a plan.

Tomorrow, I *will* get answers.

*

Eddie couldn't give me a lot of information this morning. He was still waiting on a call from Miles's attorney, but he did give me exactly what I needed.

Terrance's business card. He'd gotten it from the store, right before the police car drove off with my boyfriend inside, and he handed it over to me stealthily this morning, without a word. I knew why, too. If I caused any trouble today, he didn't want to know about it. He couldn't be any more associated with this mess than he already was—not if he had any chance of helping Miles.

Now I'm sitting in this quiet hotel suite, nursing a cold cup of coffee. Everyone else left early to catch the first flight back to L.A. No one mentioned the fact we were supposed to be on the bus on our way to Florida today. That show'd been cancelled, along with the one after. The lost shows were a silent disappointment we all shared—even me. But nobody brought it up. I'm trying to keep my hopes high that everything will be fixed soon, but the feeling in my gut says otherwise.

The clock on the wall says it's ten, and my ride should be waiting downstairs by now. The faster I get things done here in Atlanta, the faster I can be home. It's surreal. I didn't want to take this trip to begin with, and yet it feels weird that I'll be in my own bed tonight. I'll get to scratch Chord's ears and drink wine with Dee. I should be happy, but it feels like another life.

Okay, the self-pity party has officially ended. I stand up, lift my head higher, and take a deep breath. I clean out my coffee mug and collect my bag and the blue guitar. *I can do this.* It's just one more job.

Leaving the suite behind, I say a silent goodbye to my new life. With so much uncertainty ahead of me and Miles and the band, who knows if my blossoming rock star life will continue?

A black sedan idles out front. I climb into the backseat and give him the address on Terrance's business card, ignoring the pounding in my chest. Pretending I've got nerves of steel, I sit up straight and try to think of exactly what to say when I'm face-to-face with Terrance. But there's not enough time to rehearse. It feels like I merely blinked and we're here. We stop right in front of a record shop, and I realize I'm probably sitting in the same spot Miles was in when he was escorted into the police car. The anger floods back through me, and I'm no longer afraid of confronting Terrance. I let my impulses take the lead and march into the store, expecting to see him as soon as I walk in. Instead, it's some younger guy, so I slow my gait and force a smile.

"Hi. Is Terrance Young in?"

He gives me a once over and raises an eyebrow. "Yeah. He's in the back." He nods toward the other end of the store, and I walk back to find a closed door.

I knock.

"It's open," I hear him say.

Thanks for the invite. I swing the door open and when he sees me, his face—with one eye swollen and a deep gash across his right cheekbone—pales. "What the hell are you doing here?"

"Oh, good. The nice act is over. I wasn't looking forward to any more pretending."

He sits back, leaning into his chair. We're on his turf, and he thinks he's beaten us. He's mighty comfortable right now, even with the evidence of meeting Nate's fist all over his face. Nate did a number on him, but I hardly feel sympathetic. Instead, I make myself comfortable too. A chair sits against the wall near me. I push it closer to his desk and sit down across from him.

"I want you to tell me about last night's events." I've already heard it all from Nate and Eddie, but I want to see if his story matches up.

"Is this an interview?"

"I'm here for myself. Why? Do you want it on record?"

"I don't give a damn what you do. Shout it from the rooftops. It won't matter." He brings his hands together and cracks his knuckles. "But there's not much to tell. Your boy toy came in looking for a fight, got what he wanted, and paid the consequences. You did know he was on probation, right?"

I ignore his question. "From what I was told, Nate was the one who fought with you. Miles didn't touch you."

He grins and I can see precisely how the guys would've lost their temper. But Miles didn't. He'd controlled himself. "You know, it happened so fast. Could've been Nate. Could've been Miles. But I'm one hundred percent certain the right person got what he deserved. Next time—"

"What do you want from him?" This is a grown man, for god's sake. Is he really that determined to play these games?

"I want his career to go down in flames the same way mine did."

Miles did destroy Terrance's record label, but he didn't do it without reason. "You were exploiting artists. Stealing money from them. Taking advantage."

"Their naivety was not my problem. A bunch of wannabe stars signed on the dotted line without a second thought. They trusted my every word. *They* made it easy to work things to my benefit."

"And all Miles did was uncover the truth. You killed your own career."

His eyes darken and he leans forward. "And that's all I want to do," he says slowly, his voice dripping with threats. "I want the truth to come out. And when it does, no respectable label will give him the time of day just like no respectable band is walking through those doors interested in recording. Wouldn't you say that's a fair resolution to all of this?"

"Miles is already paying the consequences. Of course you know that, he's probably paying you enough in restitution to keep this store running. Did it pay for all the equipment you use too? So how about you call a truce? He's already in trouble, might be going to jail. Why can't you just leave him alone?"

He sits quietly for a moment, and I'm hopeful he's considering it. But then he shakes his head. "I have all the time in the world. Now that I know the new name he's hiding behind, it'll bring me nothing but pleasure to bring him down. You'd be wise to cut him loose. You never know when Miles's problems will affect you and your little writing career."

I stand up and glare down at him. "I will not let you ruin him. If you think I'm afraid of you, I'm not. And neither is Miles. He's innocent, and you know it." I turn toward the office door to leave but stop in the doorway and look back. Terrance is standing now, his hands casually in his pockets like he's going to be a gentleman and walk me out. I muster all of my courage to finish what I want to say. "If I have to expose you as the conniving, ruthless son of a bitch you are, I will."

In three quick steps, he's in front of me. Taken by surprise, I don't move fast enough as he grabs one of my shoulders and slams me against the doorframe. I ignore the sudden pain shooting up and down my spine, and when he sees I'm glaring at him and still not backing down, his other hand grips tight around my throat, holding me in place. Panic bursts through me. My eyes go wide. Is he insane?

"Miles may have been innocent last night, but he's hardly a saint. So what if his buddy threw the punches? He came here to start shit with me. I finished it. I hope he rots in prison this time around."

My legs are turning to jelly as I struggle to hold myself in place. Terrance's hand tightens, constricting my airway even more. I try to gasp for breath, but I can't.

He narrows his eyes. "And let me assure you, anything you try to do to me will come back to haunt you tenfold. You try to bring me down, and I'll make sure Miles, his shitty band, and his pathetic girlfriend never amount to anything in this industry. And I won't just ruin your careers. I'll ruin all your lives."

He lets me go and my shaky legs lead me toward the store's exit as fast as I can, forcing myself not to look over my shoulder. My pulse thunders, my nerves are on fire, and I feel the tears coming.

I practically leap into the car and tell the driver to start toward the airport. My words come out broken and unstable. What the hell is wrong with Terrance? He's dead set on some vindictive strategy whereas he could've rebuilt himself just as Miles did. He's not going to back down easily.

The further we get from the store, the calmer I feel. No one's ever physically threatened me like that, and I've had some intense interviews in the past—rock stars on drug binges, interviews in bad areas of town. But I've never felt unsafe. Until now.

Lucky for me, I didn't go there without a plan of my own. I run my hand through my hair, settle into my seat, and reach into my jacket pocket, pulling out the digital recorder I've had running this whole time. I press the stop button. Not only did the bastard give me permission to put everything on record and do whatever I want with it, but he flat out admitted Miles didn't hit him. What I'm holding in my hand is pure gold. It's Miles's ticket

to freedom. Terrance has no idea what's coming to him.

Chapter Eight

Miles

A cold, hard bed. Cold, hard walls. A cold, hard floor. Fuck this cell. And fuck Terrance. I've been on my best behavior since they arrested me, but inside, I'm furious. I didn't do shit to him, yet these assholes took his word over mine. Pacing back and forth in this cell is all I can do to pass time. Sitting still feels like torture. My thoughts—racing and out of control—won't organize enough to figure out what I have to do next, not that I have any control in this. The band must be pissed about the shows we're missing, but more importantly, what's Abby thinking? God, I hope she believes my side of the story. With my luck, she doesn't. She's disappointed that violence led me here again, and she's had enough. Her break up speech will probably be well written and perfectly edited. Hopefully, she'll wait until I'm out of this paper-thin blue jumpsuit to give me the inevitable, bad news.

"She's got every right to dump me," I tell my cellmate, a DUI case who showed up in the middle of the night. He's still got a hangover and has been grimacing every time I've said something out loud.

"Fuck them all, man." He rolls over on his cot and covers his eyes with one of his forearms. "Women cause all the problems. Hannah's the whole reason I landed here."

Somehow I doubt Hannah—whoever she is—made him drive the L.A. highways wasted. "Abby's not like that though. She's breathtaking. She keeps me on my toes and actually seems to give a damn about me."

"Then you're the problem." He keeps his eyes closed and scrunches his forehead to ward off the headache. "Got a good girl at home, and you screw it up. Way to go, buddy."

I stop pacing, his words a sudden wall in front of me. The drunk bastard's right. This all comes back to me. My history, the present, everything that happens in my future—it's all going to impact Abby. I've never been with anyone I've wanted to stay with, and yet staying with her means hurting her.

I fall back onto my cot and sit with my back against the wall. I bring my knees up and rest my arms on them. Shit. How'd I let all this happen? Abby doesn't deserve this. After all the effort she gave to help the band, to keep *ScandalLust* away. And in the end, I was the biggest problem. It's not like it'll just stop here. I might be able to keep myself from fighting with people, but the life I want, the life I've fought for, is filled with trouble and chaos. It's filled with the things Abby doesn't want to be a part of. And now, my sweet, beautiful woman is somewhere out there, most likely thinking of the nicest way to leave me. She'll try to make it easy for me, disguising all her own pain.

"You fall asleep over there?" my cellmate asks. "You look like you're in a trance."

"I think you're right about Abby. I'm the fuck up. Always will be."

The guy nods and slowly sits up. "Yup. Trust me on that one."

"I have to protect her, do what's right for her."

"Take it from me, it only gets worse. Gotta treat it like a bandaid, rip that sucker off. The quicker you do it, the less pain. I learned this the hard way. Tried to keep her around, begged her to stay. Everything still turned to shit, and by then, we were both broken."

This stranger is making more sense than anyone else I know. I can't be the one to break Abby. And I can't let her be the one to cause the pain.

I have to break up with her.

"Smith, you have a visitor," a guard says outside. I don't register it until he says it again. "Smith. You deaf?" I'm not accustomed to hearing my birth name anymore. Even a name as ordinary as Smith can sound foreign when you've rebranded yourself with a stage name like Miles Riot.

My head snaps in the guard's direction as he's unlocking the door. I rise to my feet, my heart in my throat. It's gotta be Abby. Eddie said they were leaving early this morning. They'd be back by now, and knowing Abby, she rushed here first. A stabbing feeling in my chest reminds me what I need to do.

My cellmate reminds me too, as I'm walking out of the cell. "Like a bandaid, man," he shouts behind me.

The guard walks me down a short hallway to a closed door. He opens it and steps aside to let me through. I squeeze my eyes shut, begging time to slow for a second so I can figure out the right thing to say to her. *I'm sorry. I can't. You deserve so much better.*

A nudge from behind says time's still passing at normal speed, and the guard isn't up for me stalling. I force one foot to move, then the other. You'd think after all the one-night stands, this would be effortless. Just another girl I'm sending home. But we all know Abby's no longer just another girl.

Inside the room, I'm equally disappointed and relieved when I see Eddie and my lawyer, Alton, sitting behind a table.

"Take a seat. We don't have a lot of time," Eddie says, pointing to a plastic white chair across the table. I sit as he continues, "How are you doing?"

"Fine."

"And they're treating you all right?"

I nod. I'm not up for talking.

Eddie turns to Alton and motions for him to start.

"You'll go before the judge tomorrow to determine if you violated your probation. Your fight with Mr. Young, being a repeat offense, is going to be considered for felony assault."

"But I didn't touch that fucker."

Alton raises a hand up to quiet me. "That's the case we'll have to make after tomorrow if the judge wants to move forward with the charges." He looks at me solemnly. "If convicted, you're most likely looking at two years at the state prison and a two thousand dollar fine."

"Two years?!"

"Afraid so."

There's no way. That'll be the end to my current life. No more music, no more touring. Hell, the stage name would vanish too. My entire identity—my future—would be ruined. Shit. Terrance really is going to get what he wants.

"If there's going to be a trial, the judge will set bail tomorrow too." Alton looks from me to Eddie and back to me. "It's not going to be chump change this time. Violating probation is $15,000 alone. Add assault, and you've got another $25,000. If they want to push it further, they can get you for stalking, which could be $20,000 on top of it."

"You're saying he won't be able to get out of here without $60,000?" Eddie slaps his hands on the table and pushes himself to standing. "He doesn't have that." He turns to me. "I'll find you a good bondsman. Don't worry. If it gets that far, we'll make sure you get your days of freedom before they go locking you up."

I'm too stunned for words. Prison time? Stalking charges? This is unbelievable. For once, I *didn't* even do it.

"Sorry, gentlemen. You know I'll do my best," Alton says. He stands up and grabs his briefcase. "I'll keep you updated," he says to me. "Is there anything else I can do for you?"

Only one thing comes to mind. "Yeah. I want one phone call before they take me back to holding."

Alton shakes my hand and leaves. Glad he's so confident. Me? I feel nothing but shock— and the urge to vomit.

Eddie pats my shoulder. "It'll be okay. We'll get you out of here. I can find the money."

"I already have the money. Don't worry about it."

"You what? I do your finances. None of you have an extra 60K to blow right now."

I scratch my nose. "Kaidan Stone paid me some money to keep drama away from his brother. You know, us fighting or the tabloids watching him or whatever."

"He what?" Eddie takes a step back and crosses his arms. "You shouldn't be accepting anything from anyone in the industry, especially without my knowledge."

"He didn't give me much of a choice. Look, it was pretty much babysitting money, and then he and Ken broke up for the umpteenth time, and he won't be back. Now it's just money burning a hole in my personal account, and it'll get me out of here. Period. You can lecture me about it later."

I walk out of the room before he can respond. My friendly guard is ready and waiting, but Alton came through, and he lets me stop at the pay phones first. "Make it quick," he says.

The urge to vomit grows even stronger as I hear the phone ring—once, twice—

"Hello?" I hear her voice, and it takes all my strength to hold it together.

"Hey." I clear my throat. "It's me," I add, as if she didn't know.

"Miles." There's a mix of joy and sadness in her tone. "How are you? God, I miss you."

I can tell her everything. How I'm feeling, what Alton and Eddie just told me, what the future looks like. But that's not why I called. I have to get to the point. Like a bandaid. "Listen. I'm sorry to have to do it this way, but I only have a minute. You and I. We have to end."

"What are you talking about?" Her voice shakes at the end, and I grip the phone tighter, hating myself for this.

"It's not a good scene for you. You can't be a part of this anymore. We can't be together."

Silence. Then she says, "You're going through a lot right now. Let's talk about all this later."

Dammit, Abby. There won't be a later. Two years in prison. What sort of monster would I be to ask her to wait for her criminal boyfriend? "I've had a lot of time to think in here, trust me. I just can't see you anymore. Sorry, but I have to go. Thanks for everything." My hand's shaking so much, I nearly miss the receiver when I hang up the phone.

I walk back to the holding cell and the guard locks me back inside. DUI guy is still here.

"You did it," he says, bluntly. My feelings must be written across my face. "It sucks, dude. I know. If you need to cry or—"

"Fuck off." I drop onto my cot and stare at the ceiling. Ugly, industrial tiles, fluorescent tube lights—I lay there, counting them, looking for patterns, trying to ignore my own thoughts. There's no need to shed tears here. It hardly relieves the pain.

Not when, on the inside, everything feels like it's being ripped apart.

* * *

Abby

Thanks for everything. Were those really the last words Miles wanted to say to me? I'm still clutching my phone in my hand, half expecting him to call again, laughing this time. Jail has to be boring. Maybe it was all a sick practical joke.

But my phone's not ringing. And I'm standing on the steps outside of the county jail. Eddie said I could meet him here and see Miles, but I was running late. My flight got in less than an hour ago, and I raced to get here. Parking took longer than I'd hoped, and I practically sprinted to get from the car to where I'm foolishly standing now. I'm out of breath and frozen. Others walk by, some giving me an irritated look for being in their way. But I can't bring myself to move. I don't want to leave, but now, I can't go inside either.

He just broke up with me.

My legs give out on me, and I sit on the step, turning to face the road. I want to believe someone else put him up to this. But he's alone in there. Plus, he's not one to give a damn what others think. So what changed between yesterday and today? How can he give up on us so easily, without even talking to me about it? He wasn't worried about us before. Does he really think I'll care about him less because of his arrest, because of the stuff that happened with Terrance?

I'm starting to feel angry. Pissed off that he'd dump me over the phone without taking two seconds to really think it through. *I've had a lot of time to think in here.* If that's the case, then did he really mean everything he said? He really doesn't want to see me again?

My mind empties. I don't know what to do.

Another body sits down next to me, and it takes me a minute before I look over and realize it's Kennedy.

"What are you doing here?" she asks me. Her usually chirpy and slightly condescending tone is gone. She's serious, solemn.

"Um," I start, but I really don't want to tell her what happened. "I'm not sure. I was going to visit Miles but I don't think he wants visitors. You?"

"Can I just say 'same'?" She sort of smiles.

I want to latch on to that tiny hint of friendliness. I feel so alone. "How are you doing?" This all has to be a pretty big blow for her.

"I've been better. Want to strangle my brother."

You and me both.

"I can't believe he let this happen," she says. "He knew he shouldn't have confronted Terrance. That guy is a sleaze. He should've backed off. Ignored him. We'd be in Florida now. Maybe at the beach. But no. We're fucking back home and dealing with more of his shit."

"Can I ask you something?"

She looks over at me.

"What happened between you two? I can't figure out your relationship. He acts like he's protective of you, but then you're fighting all the time. And then there's the whole sabotage thing where you..." I don't need to finish. She knows I'm talking about her trying to break us up. If she only knew she didn't have to do anything in the end to make that happen. Another pang in my heart reminds me of every word Miles just said to me.

She shrugs like everything between her and her brother is typical family nonsense. "He had this girlfriend awhile back. She slept with Devon. He's hated Devon ever since. I've hated every one of his whores ever since. No offense."

I laugh at the insult, too numb to care what she wants to say about me.

"If it helps, I kind of like you and him together." She pulls her hair into a ponytail and secures it with an elastic tie. "You seem to be the most normal. I'd say you keep him grounded, but he's in jail. That invalidates things."

"Too bad he dumped me." The words are out faster than I can stop them.

"Seriously?"

I nod. "He called to tell me we were over."

"Yet you're here anyway? When did he call?"

I hold my phone up. "Five minutes ago...give or take."

"Damn." She leans back, resting her elbows on the step behind her. "That sucks. You aren't going to let him go that easily though, right?"

And here I'd expected her to do cartwheels in the street. Instead, she flicks off a guy in a suit as he walks by scowling at us.

"He said he's thought it all through. Says I shouldn't be a part of this anymore. I'm not sure what more I can say to convince him otherwise. You know your brother. He's stubborn."

"And he's an idiot."

I kind of love her right this second, forgetting all the crap she's put me through.

"Listen, I've never seen Miles act like this with anyone, even that girl who screwed my boyfriend—ex-boyfriend." She scrunches her face. "He's used to others giving up on him, so he probably just cut you off before you got the chance to do the same to him. If you really love him—or whatever," she quickly corrects herself after using the "L" word, "then you won't walk away."

"Is that your plan with Devon?" If we're getting personal, then I might as well ask what she's doing about her own love life.

Kennedy thinks for a second and then smiles. "No. I think we've reached an end of an era with me and Devon. Besides, I know I'll find better."

Better than a billionaire Stone brother. I want to laugh. Last week, she would've sworn there was no better than him.

"Good for you," I say. "I hope the next guy really makes you happy."

She starts to respond but looks over her shoulder and motions for me to look too. Eddie's walking out the front door. He looks hurried and frustrated. We stand up to meet him.

"Oh, you're here," he says when he sees me. "Why didn't you come inside?"

I look at Kennedy for a second, unsure how to answer.

"She just got here," Kennedy says. "I told her your meeting was probably over. And I was right. You ready to go?" Apparently, she came here with Eddie but then couldn't find the guts to go in and face Miles.

"In a second." Eddie turns to me. "Since you weren't in there, you should know this before the tabloids somehow find out."

My pulse quickens as a wave of dread rushes through my veins. "Is it bad?"

"He's looking at two years in prison, felony assault."

"What about the tour?" Kennedy butts in.

Eddie gives her an irritated look like this should be common sense. "The tour's been cancelled. We've got bigger issues to tend to."

Kennedy lets out a huff and stomps off. I can't blame her for being pushy. Without Devon or Miles, the band's all she's got.

"He's innocent though," I say to Eddie. How can you lock up an innocent person for two years?

"It's going to be hard to prove, even with Nate's testimony. It's their word against Terrance's, and with Miles's record, the odds aren't in his favor."

I shuffle through my purse and dig out the recorder. "It's not just their word. I got Terrance on tape this morning. It's self-incriminating."

"Abby, that's not legal. You can't record a person without—"

"I asked him if he wanted it on record and he said yes. He just didn't know I was being literal. But you can hear it all on this." I thrust my hand toward him. "Take it and listen."

He accepts the tape recorder, and I can sense a small gleam of hope in his demeanor. "All right. I'll listen. I can't promise anything, but maybe Terrance will dig his own grave. That's the only real chance we've got." He pockets the recorder. "Thanks. This wasn't in your job description, I'm sure."

Nope. None of this was. "You've got that right." But this is more important to me now than any article deadline. I'm in too deep, and Kennedy's right. I can't let Miles call all the shots.

Eddie tells me the hearing's tomorrow, and we part ways as if we're going back to our ordinary lives. But nothing's ordinary anymore. I walk to my car and climb behind the wheel. Two years. Two years he'd be locked up in prison. Two years we'd be apart. No wonder Miles was letting me go. What's the point of having a girlfriend if your relationship is going to be put on hold while you serve a sentence for a crime you didn't commit?

A tear drips from my face to my hand. I didn't notice I was crying, but emotion overwhelms me and I burst out in anger and desperation. Slamming my fists against the steering wheel, I let all of my pent up frustration come out. I bawl and yell and curse the entire universe for leading me to a man I could see myself with for years to come and then taking him away. My tantrum tapers off, and I try to regroup. Deep breaths. He's not gone yet. Even Kennedy thinks I can get him back, and if things go well tomorrow, Miles won't be transferred to the state prison. But none of it's guaranteed, and the thought of it going wrong makes me sick.

Using my rearview mirror, I wipe my face and attempt to smudge my makeup back into place. I look like a mess, feel it too. Next stop, my studio. I just need to drive from here to there.

Right as I start the car, my phone rings. I answer it without looking.

"Hello there, Ms. Clarke. Polly Hemsworth here."

Dammit. *ScandalLust.* Of course. They must have their panties in a bunch over all of this.

"I'm not interested in talking to you, Polly."

"Just like you weren't interested in giving me factual information when we met. But I forgive easily." She speaks quickly, not giving me a chance to interject. "We see Miles was arrested last night and brought back to Los Angeles this morning. He's in holding until a hearing tomorrow, but word is, he's looking at doing some hard time. Can we get your side of the story on this? What went down last night? What are his charges? What's going to happen to Tempest Ultra? My measly offer of fifty thousand before can easily be doubled if we can get an exclusive with Miles's girl-friend."

At least she doesn't have all the infor-mation. Yet. There's probably someone on the inside who's more than willing to sell celebri-ty legal secrets. But not me.

"Polly," I start but she's still talking. "Pol-ly..." I say again. But she's still going on about how the money could further me and my ca-reer. "Polly!" I shout into the phone.

"Yes, Ms. Clarke?" she asks sweetly.

"Go to hell." I hang up.

Instead of driving, I pull up the *Scandal-Lust* site real quick. I forgot to check this morning, and lord knows what stories they're probably printing.

Right at the top is a picture of Miles, wide eyed as he's leaving Terrance's store. His hands are curled into fists, and he looks enraged. Behind him, Nate's been blurred out so the focus is all on Miles. A second picture shows Terrance, bruised and bloodied, made out to look like the helpless victim of an unprovoked attack. And the headline paired with it stretches across the screen in bold, red letters.

"Tempest tour screeches to a halt, Miles Riot arrested!"

Chapter Nine

Miles

Even sleep can't keep me away from my demons. Outside this cell, there's nothing good waiting for me. No more Abby. No more band. And in prison, that means no more freedom. DUI guy left this morning, and I haven't left the cot since I came back in here yesterday. I've laid here, trying to shut off all my emotions so I don't have to feel the pain and loss and disappointment. Why the hell did I go after Terrance?

Because he went after Abby first. I'd do it all again in a heartbeat.

He started this, and I finished it. Well, Nate did. But if he hadn't attacked Terrance, I know I would've. Every nerve in my body was ready to pummel him, and I would've if Nate hadn't been in the way. So whatever happens today, I willingly accept Terrance's blood on my hands. Maybe I'll flat out plead guilty while looking Terrance in the eye. Will that shmuck be in the courtroom today?

"It's time," a different guard says today. He unlocks the cell. I'm expecting chains and cuffs—seen a lot of movies—so I'm a little surprised when I'm escorted to the courtroom almost like any other normal person. The jailhouse ensemble's the only sign I'm the bad guy here.

In the courtroom, I'm directed to a table where I sit down next to my lawyer. He shakes my hand and says good morning, but I'm not interested in pleasantries. I tap my foot under the table as I nervously wait for this to get started. Glancing behind me, I spot a full room. Eddie's the only one I recognize, but with so many here to see the rock star get in trouble, I'm sure the others are just lost in the crowd.

A door opens, the bailiff appears. We're told to stand up while the judge comes in and takes his seat. Judge Emory. I remember him from before. Hopefully he's feeling generous today.

"This is the preliminary examination in the case for Terrance Young versus Matthew Smith, alias Miles Riot. The defendant is present with his attorney while Mr. Young is being represented by Mr. David Locklear." The judge adjusts the wire-framed glasses on his face and looks out at everyone, his eyes landing on mine for a second. "Let's get started.

We've been here before, gentlemen. I need to hear the events of that night, beginning with you, Mr. Locklear."

Terrance's attorney stands up to relay Terrance's story. I'm amused that cocky asshole didn't fly out here to witness this.

"My client was working in his store on the night of the incident when he received a threatening voicemail from the defendant. Minutes later, the defendant entered his office, began verbally assaulting him, and it escalated into a physical altercation. An employee called the police, and when the defendant left the store, he was arrested." Locklear shoves his hands down into his pockets. "My client confirms the attack was unprovoked, as was the first incident last year. We're seeking felony assault charges and will also be filing a suit for pain and suffering."

Every word he speaks makes me want to flip this table, fly straight to Atlanta, and inflict some *real* pain and suffering. But I keep my cool. I have no other choice.

Next up, Locklear has the voicemail played for everyone to hear. I cringe hearing my own voice, but I don't see what the big deal is. It's not like I said I was going to kill him.

"Listen carefully, you bastard. It's one thing to track me down. But to go after my girlfriend first? You've crossed a line. I'll be seeing you very soon."

Terrance was an asshole for tracking down my girlfr—Abby. I remind myself, she's not my girlfriend anymore. I hope she understands she dodged a bullet by not getting more serious with me. She's a smart woman. She'll understand.

After the voicemail ends, Terrance's attorney says he's got nothing else and sits his ass down. Now it's our turn. Alton stands and tells my side of things—how the history between me and Terrance was left in the past until the tour reached Atlanta and Terrance started sneaking around, approaching Abby behind my back. He admits my voicemail was foolish—this is why I'm letting him speak on my behalf for this hearing. I would've told him the voicemail was perfectly justified—and says while I made a vague vocal threat, I didn't follow through.

"My client was not involved in the physical altercation with Terrance Young. He stayed out of it, and the person who was involved acted out of self-defense. Terrance's threatening behavior preceding the incident escalated to face-to-face threats. When Terrance moved closer to the gentlemen in his store, they both felt physical harm was imminent. I think the evidence gathered after the event is sufficient to rule out the probable cause necessary to indict my client."

Evidence? What evidence? I look over at Terrance's guy and he's equally confused, but the judge is just as cool and collected as he's been this whole time.

"Let's play the recording," he says, and a moment later, I hear a shuffling noise. It's followed by a voice. *"Hi. Is Terrance Young in?"*

Abby. She went to Terrance's store. When? Had to have been yesterday. The audio is quiet again until I hear the sound of a door opening and Terrance say, *"What the hell are you doing here?"*

I try to contain my horror. She went after him by herself? The man's a lunatic. She should've known better.

I listen to the rest of it, my eyes focused on the wood grain of the judge's stand. Terrance took her for granted. He volunteered information, even said it could go on record. He talked about the record label, the fight. But none of it brings me relief, not when I hear what comes next. There's movement, a chair scraping across the floor, a banging noise— like a heavy weight hitting a block of wood—a gasp from Abby, and the sounds of her panicked, struggled breathing as the asshole makes even more threats, against her, against me, against my band.

I'm on my feet in an instant. "What the hell did he do to her?" I shout. The judge glares at me, a security guard rushes over, and Alton quickly pushes me down, back into my seat.

Not now, his eyes seem to scream at me.

I could kill the fucker. He dared to touch her. He's lucky he's not here. I'd break every one of his fingers. Prison would be welcome if it meant ensuring he can never hurt her again.

I'm still fuming, my whole body tense, when Alton tells the judge he's finished. The judge announces a five-minute recess while he makes his decision.

"But you stay seated right where you are, Mr. Smith," he tells me. "No more outbursts from you."

Like a scorned child, I slouch in my seat and wait. There's noise behind me as people come and go, but my thoughts are in one place. Abby. How could she be so damn stupid to go to Terrance with no one there to protect her? This is what I mean. This is why we can't be together. She might be okay with living life as a rock star's girlfriend, but I'm not okay with it. I can't let her put herself in danger on my behalf ever again. And I won't. This is why we broke up. DUI guy had it right. Being with me means bringing her down and fucking up her whole life. She never would've gone to Terrance if it weren't for me.

The judge returns, the room goes silent, and I wait to hear what's next for me. I hate not being in control of my life, having others tell me where I'll be five minutes from now, where I'll sleep tonight, how I'll spend the next years if I'm convicted.

"Let's not waste any time," Judge Emory says. "Matthew Smith, you voluntarily contacted Mr. Young, threatening him. You followed that by confronting him at his place of business. Both actions are a violation of your probation."

Fuck. This is it. Even with Terrance proving he's an asshole, I'm still going down for this.

"However," the judge says, "the recording of Mr. Young brings new revelations about the previous case. Had it been available last year, your charges may have been very different. There's a possibility you wouldn't have been on probation at this time had the jury been aware of this knowledge during last year's trial. With that in consideration, the court will not be moving forward with a trial. Your probation will be reviewed, and if deemed necessary, a hearing will be set to modify the current terms."

Does that mean no prison time?

"Let's move on to the alleged stalking. Prosecution does not have sufficient evidence to prove probable cause. If anything, Mr. Young could be countersued for the same infringement. And finally, the assault. It's clear Mr. Young was physically attacked and bodily harm was inflicted."

But... Tell me there's a but.

"Mr. Young, had he been here today, may have been able to shed light on his own story.

According to the police report, Mr. Matthew Smith caused the bodily harm. According to the defendant, it was another party acting in self-defense. If that's all I had to go on, then we'd go to trial. But in the recording, legally attained by a third party, Mr. Young not only demonstrated his own apt for violence, but he admitted Matthew Smith, alias Miles Riot, was not the aggressor. The charges are dropped."

An enormous breath of relief escapes me. That's it, right? Those were the charges. They're all being dropped. I'm good to go.

"This is a difficult situation for me," Judge Emory says. "I'd love to end this case here and now, but the new evidence complicates things. Mr. Locklear..."

I turn to see Terrance's attorney pale.

Judge Emory continues, "Your client will appear in my courtroom at the date and time set forth after this hearing adjourns. Last year's case will be reconsidered, and you'll have sufficient time to build a defense against the audio recording we heard here today. Your client will receive a fair trial, but let me assure you, his actions against the third party who attained that recording were violent, malicious, and deplorable. You can tell him I said so myself." He turns back to me. "You're free to go, Mr. Smith. Stay out of trouble."

The hearing's adjourned, and I'm in shock. Alton tells me he'll keep in touch about the next court dates, but it hardly fazes me. Not only will it not get any worse for me, but now I have the chance to see Terrance get a dose of his own medicine. This couldn't have ended better.

A slap on my back snaps me back to attention. It's Nate. I throw my arms around him in a bear hug. "We did it, man."

"I'm so fucking glad you aren't going to become someone's boyfriend in prison," he says.

I push him back. "Fuck you too."

Dax is there, confused but happy. "I don't know what the hell's going on, so you better be ready to explain yourself when we get out of here."

Eddie and Kennedy come up next. Kennedy, tears in her eyes, hugs me tight. "I was so scared for you."

I think she means it. I hug her back. "Everything's fine."

Eddie tells me I got really lucky, and as they all disperse, I see Abby behind them. She's there with another girl I don't recognize. When they walk up, I notice Abby keeps her distance. Ice runs through my veins as I remember all I've put her through.

"This is my good friend, Dee," she says, and Dee shakes my hand.

"You didn't have to come," I tell Abby, trying not to sound like a complete jerk, but she's also the one who saved my ass. "Thank you though. For what you did, even though I wish you hadn't. Terrance could have—"

"The *thank you* is enough. Don't worry about what I did." Her voice is flat, maybe even angry. "Glad it worked out for you."

She's looking at me like she expects me to say something else. What does she want? For me to take everything back? Tell her things can go back to normal now that I'm not going to be stuck in the slammer for two years? No. This was a close enough call. I'm not dragging her further into my life. It's not good for her. We can't be together. Period.

After a moment of me not saying anything, she drops her shoulders. "Well, I'm going to go. See you—or you know. Good luck with everything." She and Dee leave. I watch her walk away, ignoring the crushing pain in my chest. I want to run after her. A part of me feels like I *need* her. But...I can't. She doesn't deserve this. She stops and says something to Kennedy, and then they're gone.

Fuck. This may have been the last time I see her.

*

An hour and a half later, I'm back in my normal clothes, pulling into the apartment I rent with Nate and Dax—princess Kennedy insisted on having her own place. The extravagance of the fancy tour bus and hotel accommodations was cool and all, but damn, it's good to be home in my shitty little place near the beach. If we're ever lucky enough to be signed, because fuck knows what's going to happen now—the paps were everywhere when I left county—we might relocate to a bigger place, but I'm not sure I want some rich boy palace. No, scratch that. I *know* I don't want it. Picture Devon Stone's place. I can only imagine what it must be filled with, besides drugs.

I've got a smirk on my face as I race up the steps to the second floor. Third door on the left. Apartment 325. I throw it open and a range of noise bombards me as I find it filled with the band and a bunch of people I actually recognize—big difference from the parties on tour. Dax comes over first and thrusts a beer bottle into my hand.

"Welcome home, asshole."

I take a swig and look around. You'd almost think the tour, the arrest, never happened. It's just another house party hosted by some rambunctious rockers. Music plays from the stereo—a woman's vocals, definitely not Ken's, put me in a trance as I push through the group and make my way into my apartment. Some people are dancing or standing off to the side drinking, but most are clustered around Tempest members, probably getting as much of a story as they can from them. As I near a couch, ready to collapse, a hand grips my arm.

"Hey stranger."

I turn to see an old friend, Sindy—yeah, she changed the spelling on purpose. A goth chick, short, spunky. We used to hook up, but that ended a while ago.

"How's it going?" I ask her, being nice.

"I heard you've been on quite the adventure." Her nose ring sparkles as she talks. "I'd like to hear about it." The sly smile on her face implies she's not interested in talking at all. I've been through this routine with her many times.

I smile and try to find my old self—the guy who'd screw who he wanted, when he wanted, no strings attached. "Maybe later," I tell her. That guy's not me anymore, and even talking to her, knowing what she's wanting, feels wrong. The old game doesn't interest me anymore. Where once it was the highlight of most my nights, just the thought is empty and shallow to me.

Dammit. And I know why, too. No other woman will be able to compare to—to her.

"I gotta borrow him for a second," Nate says, appearing out of nowhere and leading me toward the back door without an explanation.

He pushes me out onto the small balcony where Dax and Kennedy are waiting. He closes the door behind us and joins the other two.

"I'm glad you're out. Things could've gone to hell today," Nate says, and I nod in agreement. "But I stood up for you without knowing why the fuck I was standing up for you. Today, at the hearing, the judge called you Matthew, said you'd been there before. So if you want to enjoy your homecoming party, you better start talking now. We all deserve to know what happened." He looks over at Dax, who's clearly in agreement. Then at Kennedy, who's pretending she's just as clueless.

I glare at her but let it go. It doesn't matter, and Nate's right. He saved my ass. He should know.

So I tell them everything. About my real name and why I changed it. About the label I brought down and the legal battle that came after it. There's no use hiding it anymore. Plenty of people who sat in the courtroom today went home to put pieces together. Hell, *ScandalLust* probably had someone in there. I'd be an asshole to make these guys the last to know.

"You're telling me Eddie's your probation officer? How could he not say anything? What the hell is he doing managing us?"

"You could say, he found his calling when he met us."

The guys don't know what to think, that much is obvious.

Dax pipes in, "We're supposed to be brothers, and you didn't tell us you were on probation. All the stupid shit we've done, it could've landed you in jail how many times?"

"Eddie was looking out for—"

"Fuck him. And fuck you," Nate says. "We would've looked out for you."

He storms back inside, and I expect Dax to do the same. They're right, you know. I should've just told them. But the information was sensitive. The fewer people who knew, the better. I explain this to Dax while he's still standing in front of me. I don't mention that Kennedy knew all along. She can tell them if she wants, but there's no use having them pissed at her too.

Dax is considering what I've said when the door opens again. Out comes Nate, this time a bottle of whisky in one hand and a stack of shot glasses in the other.

"Enough. Fuck it all," he says and looks me in the eye. "Trust your brothers, okay? No more hiding shit. Now let's leave the past to rot with that Terrance prick."

He hands us each a glass and clumsily pours the whisky into them.

"To brotherhood," Dax says, then looks at Kennedy. "Can you just be a dude to make this easy?"

She laughs. "To brotherhood."

We clink the glasses together and gulp down the liquor. It's like silk, warming me from the inside. Everything's turning out all right.

Well, almost everything.

We head back inside, and I sneak away to my room to sort through my thoughts. It's been an overwhelming couple of days, and the chaos of a party isn't going to help any.

I open my door and stop breathing. Abby's sitting on my bed.

"Don't be mad," she says. "Kennedy told me to come. I just want to talk."

I consider having a heartfelt discussion with her for all of two seconds. No, that's not what I want, and I'm sure it's not what she wants either. I close the space between us, slamming the door behind me in the process. When I reach her, sitting on the bed, I kneel down, cup her face in my hands, and kiss her hard. She stifles a gasp before opening her mouth to me. Her arms loop around my neck, holding me as if she's afraid to let go. I help her move back in my bed and lay her head down on the pillows, the whole time, not letting our kiss end. When I pull away, I see her breathing heavy and gazing up at me. She's beautiful. She's perfect. What the hell am I doing?

I was so convinced I was nothing but a problem to her. I could ruin her life. But maybe I won't. Today was a close call, but the other day at Terrance's, I restrained myself. I don't have to be some reckless criminal. I can be whoever Abby needs me to be. I *want* to be that guy for her.

"I'm so sorry about everything," I tell her, my voice low. "I don't want to hurt you."

"Then don't." She's blunt, but the smile on her face is sexy and flirty. "You aren't getting rid of me that easily. Not after making me fall for you the way you did."

"I think I could love you," I say, the words escaping me. Oh well. I just toasted the band to no more lying, and this is as true as ever.

"Me too," is all she says before my mouth finds hers again.

I fumble with her shirt, a green, plaid button down. The buttons snap, and I rip them apart, revealing a lacy black bra. I kiss the exposed skin of her breasts while peeling her shirt off of her and tossing it to the floor. She tugs at the hem of my t-shirt. I sit up and yank it off, letting it join hers. Abby pulls herself up, standing on her knees. Without breaking eye contact, she unbuttons her jean shorts and pulls them off. The second she's in nothing but her underwear, I grip her hips and lie back, pulling her down on top of me. She squeals, then laughs. Outside, the music is still blaring.

Seeing her face light up, I can't help but smile. I'm a dumbass for thinking I could just let her go.

"What do you think's going to happen at your next hearing?" she asks.

I don't mind talking business when we're half naked. In fact, I prefer it. "Hopefully, Terrance's words come back to haunt him. Did he hurt you?" I ask, remembering what I'd heard on the recording.

She shakes her head. "Just scared me, but I'm a big girl." She kisses me. "And it was worth it."

"To think, that bastard thought he'd beat us at his little game. Here we are, getting the last laugh."

Her eyes go wide. "That's it!"

"What?"

She sits up again, and it takes everything not to pull her back down, her gorgeous body taunting me.

"We have to beat him at his game."

"But we already did," I remind her.

"No." She's in another world now, and, worse, she's climbing off of me, off of the bed. "He still has time to leak everything to the press, to present you as a risk to the other labels. We have to beat him to it."

I sit up. "What are you saying?"

"Do you trust me?" she asks plainly.

Amused that she's clearly got a plan spinning in her head, I say, "Of course," because I do.

"Then I have to go."

Go? Where? Seriously? She sees the disappointment on my face.

"Don't worry," she tells me. "I'm not going to do anything stupid. But you have to let me take the reins on this one. I think I can save you *and* the band. I'm sure of it."

She quickly dresses and then leaves. I fall back into the bed—so much more comfortable than a jail cell cot. Abby thinks she can save me. Funny girl. She already has, and not just from a nasty trial, but from myself. The old Miles. The one I don't need to be anymore, not with her around.

Chapter Ten

Abby

"You look like you didn't sleep last night," Dee tells me. She stayed at my studio last night to make sure I was okay. No matter how many times I reassured her, she didn't believe me.

"That guy choked you. He threatened you," she had said, as if I didn't remember.

"Yup. But I'm alive and well, aren't I?"

"Then your boyfriend dumped you out of nowhere."

"We're back together, so it doesn't matter. It was just a moment of uncertainty." Everything she listed that was supposed to prove I was some bruised and broken girl ended up being the same things that made me feel confident and capable. I felt strong, not vulnerable. Alive, not defeated. Things couldn't be better.

But she's right this morning. I didn't sleep last night. I pulled an all-nighter, writing the most important article of my career. And in the early hours, I called Jonathan, royally pissing him off. But I got it approved, and it would be published in the next couple hours. My nerves were a wreck knowing soon, everyone would know the truth about Miles. But we were the ones in control. We were calling the shots. It wasn't Terrance spilling the story. Better yet, it was being published in Lydian, so it was credible, not some tabloid B.S.

I haphazardly got dressed, Chord following me around, wagging his tail. He was happy I was home, but I felt bad. I hadn't had more than a few minutes to greet him. I'd get him to the dog park this afternoon. That would make up for it.

"So tell me what his place is like. His room. I can't believe you're dating a rock star." Dee's making coffee and talking a mile a minute.

"Surprisingly typical." When I got to Miles's, it was already filled with people, so I didn't get a good look at it, but his room was empty—hence the reason I was hiding out in there. I wasn't in a partying mood when I'd gotten there. I was scared to death Miles would be mad at me, would make me leave. But I trusted my gut, and hell, I trusted Kennedy. And it paid off far easier than I thought. One look at me, and he was on top of me, kissing me, apologizing. He couldn't disguise his feelings for me if he tried.

"Earth to Abby." Dee's waving her hand in my face.

I refocus on my surroundings and smile at her. "He's a normal guy. Mismatched furniture, dirty clothes on the floor." I grab my makeup bag and start making my face look a little more awake.

"And you're falling head over heels for him," Dee yells from the kitchen.

My silence is all the response she needs. When I return for my coffee, she's sitting on a bar stool talking to Chord. "You're going to have a new daddy."

I slap her playfully on the arm and climb onto the stool next to her, accepting my fresh mug of caffeine. Last night was rough. I had to word everything just right. I don't want anyone getting the wrong impression of Miles, and everything I shared...let's just say it's going to surprise plenty of readers and Tempest fans.

"I'm sorry to drink and run," I say, chugging the hot coffee as fast as I can. "But I have to get going." I want to be at Miles's before the article is posted.

She wishes me luck, and I hurry out.

Yesterday, the apartment was crowded, noisy, boisterous. Today, it's eerily quiet, somber. When Miles lets me in, he kisses me sweetly. Then we join everyone else—Kennedy, Dax, Nate, and Eddie—in the living room. No groupies. No lit joints. No alcohol, surprisingly—even I feel like we may need it.

I check my watch. "Almost time." There's no need to announce it, but I needed to fill the silence.

"I hope you know what you're doing," Kennedy says, opening a laptop decorated in stickers. Her tone is equally hopeful and threatening. I can't imagine how she may act out if this all goes downhill.

"It'll be okay. No matter what." I take Miles's hand and interlock my fingers with his. His hands, strong and a little calloused from guitar playing, bring me security. "What's important is—"

"It's up!" she shouts, interrupting me. "*What's a Rock Star Without a Dark Side*— nice title. And look at the photo." She laughs a little and turns the screen our way so we can see the one I picked out. It's from the shoot they did in Dallas, Miles leaning against the classic car, his guitar hanging from his shoulder. He's hot, filled with charisma, yet hints at being a little vulnerable. It's the precise tone I needed to set for the article that follows. Kennedy starts reading it. "Matthew Smith is an extraordinary man. Miles Riot is an extraordinary rock star. What you don't know is this: They're the same person. So why did Miles erase Matthew and his infamous past? A trail of lies, exploitation, and an explosive fallout sets the scene, and if this were an action movie, Miles Riot/Matthew Smith is the fearless hero who sacrificed everything to take down the corporate enemy."

She takes a breath, nodding her head subtly as though she's approving my opening. When she continues, she reads faster. It's everything we already know, starting with Miles's old band and label. I introduce Terrance and the ways he took advantage of new bands, I explain how they all pulled their contracts using a loophole, and I follow it with the fight that landed Miles on probation to begin with. Before Kennedy moves on to the final paragraphs, Eddie's phone rings. He stands up to take the call, and we sit, frozen, not knowing what to expect. When he returns, he throws the phone into the couch. It bounces off the cushion and clatters to the ground. Eddie spins on his heel, tugs his fingers through his hair, and then slams a hand into the wall.

"Talk," Miles says.

Eddie comes back to the group and drops onto the couch. "Rev Records just pulled their offer. Apparently, Xavier was once a buddy of Terrance's. He didn't know you were the same guy who took down Graffiti, but now that he knows, he's not interested."

"But did he read the *entire* article?" I ask. This matters. If my final words didn't make a difference, then...

"They all read it. They called a meeting as soon as they saw the headline so they could make a decision. It was a quick one, obviously. They're out." He sighs and shakes his head. "Finish reading it, Kennedy."

She does. "Our hero may have won the battle against the corrupt record company, but his actions did not come without consequences. Those consequences have impacted everything important to him—his family, his love life, and most of all, his band. Tempest Ultra started as an experiment to see if Miles could handle collaborating with his little sister. Not only did the pair work, the band as a whole has exploded in talent and potential. Now the big name labels are after them. The media is in a frenzy. And the future for Tempest Ultra is promising." Kennedy pauses and takes a deep breath before continuing. I grip Miles's hand stronger. "In a world of uncertainty, our hero knows his dark past is one that can follow him forever. Tempest will rise. They will be every bit the international sensation they've set out to be. But in honor of the band, and not tarnishing their identity, Miles Riot will not be continuing as the band's guitarist and backing vocals. He respectively and humbly resigns, knowing whoever will take his place will have the opportunity of a lifetime. Who knows what tomorrow holds for our rock star, but his past is far from regrettable and his future is sure to be nothing less than remarkable. The legacy of Miles Riot will forever be alive."

Last night, when I was in the middle of this article, Miles called me. It was at an ungodly hour, but he'd sounded awake and alert. "I'm quitting the band."

"What are you talking about?" I'd asked.

"I just talked to the others. They aren't happy, but they get it. All this drama. The problems we may have getting signed. It's because of me. Remove me from the formula, and there's no reason for the labels to ditch them."

"That's insane, Miles. You're a major part of Tempest. You can't just leave." All this work so he could have a career and he's just going to abandon it?

"I already did. It's done. So you should print it. Make it widely known. It'll protect them, and we'll still get to call out Terrance for what he is. Believe me when I say this is the right idea."

"But are you okay? This is your life."

"It's not *all* of my life. I've got you, right?"

I smile. "Yeah."

"Then I'm okay."

*

Kennedy shuts the laptop and looks up at Miles. "You're an idiot."

"Maybe. But it might work."

Nate shakes his head. "Rev barely finished reading before they pulled their offer. We're fucked man. Whether or not you're in the band, we're fucked." He gets up and goes to the kitchen. See? I knew we needed alcohol to get through this.

Dax remains silent, but his demeanor proves he's unhappy. His jaw is tightly set, and he stares off into space.

What's going to happen to them all? If they don't get signed, if the band breaks up, what then? It seems so unfair, to everyone.

Eddie's phone rings. My heart stops. I shouldn't have written the article. It's all my fault. I thought the truth would be the honorable thing to do, that people would respect it. But what if I was horribly wrong? The phone rings again. Eddie grabs it off the floor and looks at its display. The room feels thick, the walls closing in.

"It's Kaidan Stone."

Two Months Later

Abby

My doorbell rings, and Chord barks, racing through the living room.

"Gotta go, Dee. He's here." I'm still wrapped in a towel, and my hair's a mess on my head. Oh well. He's seen me worse.

"You guys have fun," Dee says. We hang up, and I toss the phone onto my bed before letting Miles in.

"Wow," he says after taking a good look at me and closing the door behind him. He's holding a big box in his hand. "Never mind what's in here." He tosses the box on the floor and pulls me toward him. "You can wear this tonight." He wraps his arms low around my hips, one hand cupping my ass, and he kisses me for a good, tasty minute. His touch, his smell, his taste. It'll never get old.

As much as I'd love to drop the towel and let him have his way... "We're going to be late."

He lets me go and recovers his box. "This is for you." He hands it to me.

I open it, to find a large package wrapped in purple tissue paper. Uncovering it, I pull out a gorgeous gown, it's floor length, black layers of chiffon. The bodice is lined with crystals that glisten as I turn it around, checking out the back—there's barely a back there. "Miles, it's beautiful."

"It has to be beautiful to be good enough for you."

Though a little cheesy, his compliment makes me swoon. The dress really is perfect. It's equally classy and racy. I love it. I go to my wardrobe and find the perfect thong to wear underneath, giving Miles a wink when I pull it out. Then I close myself in the bathroom to get dressed without any interruptions. There's no way a bra would work with this gown, but once it's on, I see there's plenty of support built in to make a bra obsolete. In fact, it flatters my body better than I could've hoped. Looking in the full-length mirror on the back of the bathroom door, I spin around to check out the back. The dress stops just short of the elastic for my thong. It's a little sexy. The skirt dances around my legs as I move, and I can't believe how comfortable it is. Miles chose wisely.

There's still the mess of my hair and makeup to deal with, but before I can pull out my makeup bag, there's a knock on the door. "Give me a minute, Miles."

"Actually, my name's Trish Martinez. I've been brought in to give you the full star treatment."

I force my jaw closed as I open the door. A woman stands there holding a big silver case and smiling. I glare at Miles. "Are you serious?"

He laughs. "Get used to it."

I relent and go to the dining room, sitting down in a chair, and letting Trish take over.

"I thought you weren't into the glitz and glam," I say to Miles in an accusatory tone.

"You don't see me getting all dolled up."

But he is, in Miles's sense. He's wearing a full-blown tux and his shoes are even shined. His hair's still a little messy, but I can tell he showered this morning. He looks damn good.

Trish finishes my makeup, keeping it simple, and then moves onto my hair. She curls it and pins it to one side, gathering what's left hanging into an intentionally messy bun. After securing it, she sprays me with a gallon of hairspray and then hands me a mirror.

My smoky makeup brings attention to my eyes. She went with pink for my lips to make me look more sweet than sexy. And my up-do is magazine-worthy. You better believe I'll try to recreate it on my own some other time. But even I'll admit I look good. I look confident. I look alluring.

I look like a rock star's girlfriend.

*

The car pulls up to a big iron gate, and a security guard lets us pass. We end up in a long line of cars, all leading to the same place—an enormous mansion positioned right on the Pacific Coast. I've tried getting interviews here before to no avail. Yet here we are, pulling up, welcome guests on a list of hundreds. This is surreal. An usher opens the door for us, and we climb out. I loop my arm around Miles's elbow and clutch a small black bag in my other hand.

"This is it," I say.

Miles kisses the top of my head. "I'm ready if you are."

We climb the steps to the wooden French doors. A security guard in a suit recognizes us and opens the door without bothering to check the list. This is the closest to red carpet treatment that I've had...ever. I'm loving it.

We go inside and find ourselves in a wide-open foyer. Two sets of stairs lead the way to the second floor, and a massive "S" monogram is inset in the tiled floor we're standing on. The Stone mansion is every bit as glamorous as you'd think.

"There you are!" Kaidan Stone spots Miles and casually walks our way. A server with a tray of drinks passes him, and Kaidan quickly grabs two glasses, handing one to each of us. "Welcome. The rest of the band is that way." He points toward a hallway that opens into a ballroom of some sort.

"Thanks," Miles says. "Before I miss a chance to say this, I just want you to know I appreciate the second chance."

That ominous day at the apartment, we sat there frozen, certain the band's career was over. Kaidan called, Eddie took the phone out onto the balcony. Ten minutes felt like ten hours. But then he came back in with the greatest news imaginable. "Stone Records isn't backing down. They're ready for you to sign when you are. But on one condition..."

Kaidan throws a fake punch at Miles's shoulder. "You really thought you could just leave the next big rock band? We wanted Tempest. You're part of Tempest."

"But everything I did to Graffiti."

Kaidan bursts out with a laugh. "You may have been able to take down some tiny, no-name company, but believe me, you couldn't put a dent in the Stone Empire if you tried. Not that you'll ever feel the need to try. We're going to treat you like royalty."

It explains the dress and makeup artist Miles brought to my place. If he's being thrown into rock star royalty, then consider me his queen. And the kingdom is certainly going to flourish. Last week, Miles had another hearing—the last one, if luck works out. His probation was excused once he paid the final installment of restitution to Terrance. What would've been over a million dollars in total, I learned, was reduced to $200,000— the cost of the loss of company, minus the predicted loss they endured from losing all the signed bands. Basically, Terrance lied to the bands, the bands rightfully left, and Miles was simply a catalyst to help the bands see they were being exploited and ripped off. Somehow, Miles was able to pay the direct order to Terrance without flinching. I don't know how he did it. If I had to pay that much...it would be impossible. But it doesn't matter now. He's completely free. Terrance was found guilty of company fraud, of stalking me, and of making death threats. He's in a cell right now waiting on his own bail hearing. I'm not one to be spiteful, but I don't feel sorry for him. Like he said, the right person got exactly what he deserves. And Miles? He's back in his band where he belongs, and the band is an official headliner on Stone Records. Judging by this party being thrown for them, things are only going to get better from here.

Miles shakes Kaidan's hand, thanks him again, and we head toward the ballroom. The entire space is exquisitely decorated with black leather sofas, satin tapestries, and a big stage set up in front of the large glass doors looking out at the ocean. Hanging behind the stage is a massive banner. A group photo of the band is printed along with the words "Tempest Ultra" in bold, scribbled letters at the top—their official logo. To the side of the stage, I spot Kennedy, wearing a vibrant red dress. She stands out more than anyone else here, and on her arm is a new guy. I'd heard about him, Kennedy's new boy toy, but I hadn't seen him yet. He's older than her, and I can see he's got a nice smile. Here's to hoping things work out better in this relationship. It would be nice to see Kennedy stable for more than a few days. Kennedy's face gleams with a huge smile, and when guests move out of the way, I see she's talking to Devon. *Oh boy.* What's her game plan here—introduce the ex to the new guy? Test Devon to see if he blows a gasket and pummels the boyfriend? But Devon doesn't look pissed or jealous or anything. He shakes the new guy's hand and talks to him like they're old pals. I'm watching in anticipation, waiting for something explosive to happen, but eventually Devon nods a good-bye and walks away. His face once he turns his back on them tells me exactly what he thinks about Kennedy and her new relationship. He's relieved. She was right. It really is the end of an era for those two, and the timing couldn't be better now that the band is signed to Stone. It should be a good sign that all the drama of the past is over.

Party guests continue to file in, and I start spotting faces I recognize—not because I know them, but because I've seen them in my own magazine. These are the big guns, and

Miles and the band are a part of it now. It's unbelievable how everything worked out. And not just for them...

My bag starts vibrating, and I dig out my phone to see Jonathan calling. I excuse myself from the party and return to the foyer to take the call.

"Hello, my feature editor." Ever since the article paid off and saved Tempest's career, Jonathan's kept me busy, saying I've set a new standard.

"What can I do for you?" I nonchalantly start up the curved staircase.

"Oh, are you too busy being a professional to have a friendly conversation?"

"Please," I say. "How often do you call for a mere casual conversation? You've got work for me to do, and knowing you, you're going to try to assign me to something far out of my comfort zone." Again... I want to add. But it all led me to Miles, so I'm up for any challenge he wants to send me now.

"I don't think there's anything you aren't bold enough to do at this point." I appreciate the flattery and sit down in a lounge area upstairs. It's like everything about this mansion is set up for hospitality and comfort. "But really, I called to tell you good luck."

"Good luck? Why's that?"

"Because your phone's been ringing off the hook at the office. Agents wanting you to interview their clients. Managers wanting you to tour with other bands. And job opportunities like you wouldn't believe."

Job opportunities?

Jonathan doesn't wait for me to ask. At some point in our history, I admitted to my real dreams, writing for Unwired Press, getting the chance to go back home. "They called. They're ready for you. More than ready judging by the salary they want to throw at you. I can't compete, so all I can do is wish you good luck and hope you don't forget about us little people."

This could be it. I could go back to Texas. I could see my family more. I can work in the setting I've only dreamed of for years. It could all be real. But then I look around this mansion. I think of how far I've come right here in L.A., and I think of Miles and how promising our future is together. There's only one place that's my home right now.

"I think I'd like to stay right where I am," I tell Jonathan.

"You sure?" he asks, and I half expect him to force me to quit, make me follow my dreams. But what he doesn't know is, I already am. I'm living a dream, and I don't want to wake up yet.

"I'm positive, as long as you'll let me stay."

"You bet your ass you can stay. Don't party too hard tonight. I expect you here bright and early in the morning."

We hang up, and I'm still smiling when I see Miles reach the top of the stairs.

"You hiding out on me?" He smiles sweetly and I wait for him to get close enough, grab his arm, and pull him down next to me. My lips crush into his, our tongues dancing. I feel one of his hands at my knee, and then it slowly slides up my thigh. There's far too much fabric between us. I push him back and stand up.

"Everything all right?" he asks.

"More than all right." I take his hand and lead him down the first hallway, the first door I find. It's clearly a guest room, perfectly decorated yet obvious no one lives in here. I pull Miles inside with me and close the door, leaning against it and looking up at him. My eyes must say everything—well, that and my blatant invitation after bringing him into an empty bedroom.

He kisses me, his hair tickling my cheek. Savoring his taste, I push him back toward the king sized bed. He pulls me along with him, and when we reach the bed, he spins us around and pushes me onto the plush mattress. My clutch falls from my hand. I hear it hit the floor. Miles is on me in a mix of fevered passion and desperate adoration. I love the way he looks at me, like I'm the only human that exists on this planet. Breathing heavy, he kisses my forehead, my earlobe, my neck. I spread my legs to invite him closer. My dress moves without constriction, making me love it even more in this moment. I grab at Miles's tux jacket and push it off his shoulders. He lets it slide off his arms and onto the bed next to us. Then he grabs his tie, loosening it while I fumble at his buttons, exposing sexy tattooed skin as each one comes unfastened. As I work to undress him, I watch him watching me. He takes in my eager gaze, my heaving breasts, the exposed skin around the top of the bodice. He stands up to ditch his pants and boxers, and I feel like a goddess— dressed like a fashion model while Miles is right next to me, completely naked. His smooth skin wraps tightly around the muscles of his arms, his chest, his stomach, dipping into the crevices between his abs. My fingers twitch, wanting to explore every inch of his firm body. And he very clearly wants me, too. His hardness ready and waiting.

I look up at him from under my long lashes and give him a half smirk. "Well, what are you waiting for?"

He smiles—a real smile, and I melt. With any luck, I'll get to spend the rest of my life making this man happy. Miles practically dives onto me, burying his face in the curve of my neck. I feel a nibble as his hands grab ahold of the straps of my dress and slide them off my shoulders. He slowly pulls it off my body, moving away from me along with it. My skin prickles from the sudden cool air as the dress puddles into a pile on the floor beneath my feet. Miles reaches down and grabs my clutch, finding the condom I'd put in it earlier. By the time he's ready for me, I'm squirming, aching for him. He looks down at me, only my thong and black strappy heels left on. Then he kneels down and kisses the space where my thigh meets my hip. I arch my back, begging him to do more, to have his way with me. His lips still on my skin, he looks up at me, a mischievous look on his face. He takes the elastic of my thong between his teeth, and tugs my panties off without using his hands, leaving my heels on. On his way back up, he leaves a trail of kisses on my calf, past my knee, going up, all the way to the apex of my thighs. His tongue flicks the sensitive folds of skin and I move my legs further apart. Hands rub my skin along my hips and up toward my breasts, where he cups them in his strong hands. His thumbs circle my nipples while his mouth tastes the heat of my sex. Bursts of pleasure rush through me, and a moan escapes me. He doesn't stay down there long though. He kisses my clit, then my stomach, then my breasts, before meeting my lips again. His mouth is hot with need. I wrap my legs around his waist, and in one swift motion, he buries himself into me. I cry out. God, he feels so good. We quickly find a rhythm, hard and fast. His eyes—dark and intense with lust—watch me as I throw my head back, not bothering to keep quiet at this point. Everyone should be downstairs anyway. Through it all, I can still hear some of the party. Someone's speaking at a microphone, talking about the band, I guess. Miles keeps driving himself into me, harder with each thrust, and my muscles clench around him, feeling every inch of unabated bliss. I seek out something to grab onto, a pillow, a blanket, Miles's back. I claw my nails into him, and hear him let out a growl. He kisses and sucks at my neck and shoulder, not being gentle anymore. His teeth graze my skin, and a thrill rushes through me. A thrill that says our sex life is only going to get more adventurous with time. Hell, our entire relationship will.

Downstairs, I hear cheering before a louder voice, undoubtedly Kennedy's says, "As soon as we get our guitarist out here..." There's more excitement than annoyance in her voice.

"Oh my god. Are you supposed to be performing?" I ask Miles. Talk about poor timing.

He grins, but doesn't stop. Instead, he lifts me up with him until he's sitting on the bed and I'm straddling him. Before coming down on top of him, I pause. "Are you?"

"I'm not leaving this room until you come for me," he says, not a single hint of humor in his voice. It's hot.

I thrust myself down onto his hard length, our bodies pressed together as I rise and fall. His hands scratch down my back, landing on my ass as he supports me, making me move faster for him. My arms hug his neck, his face buried in my breasts, as I feel every muscle in my body tense. A warmth seeps through my veins, settling at my core.

"That's right," he says to me as my body starts to tremble. It feels too intense. It's too much, but I keep riding him, letting every sensation take over me.

"Come for me," he growls.

I scream out as the first waves of pleasure crash through me. We keep moving together as another wave hits, then another. I bite into

his shoulder as the peak of my orgasm over-
takes me like an unrelenting storm. He pushes me down harder onto him and lets out a
groan as he experiences his own release. He
thrusts again, emptying himself into me. We
sit there for a second, trying to catch our
breath. A drum solo from downstairs snaps us
out of it, and Miles pulls me off of him, grabs
his clothes and disappears into the bathroom
for a minute. I take the opportunity to get
dressed and check my hair in a mirror. It's a
little out of place, so I fix the pins to make its
disheveled appearance look...intentional.

Miles comes out of the bathroom, and I
smile at him. He's dressed again, but he's
ditched the tie and the top buttons of his tux
are undone.

"You're going to go out looking like that?"
I ask. But he doesn't answer. He kisses me one
last time, shoves his tie into my clutch, hands
it to me, then opens the door and leaves.

I follow behind him as he casually descends
the staircase and pushes his way back into the

party, through the crowd. I stop short of the stage. He jumps onto it, right as Kennedy approaches her microphone. Nate's already playing the bass line when Miles grabs his guitar and slings it around his neck. Dax's drumbeat picks up, and Miles starts strumming without missing a single note. It's like he was on stage, ready the whole time, a seamless transition from being with me upstairs to performing in front of this group. I'm still coming down from that orgasm, and from the way Miles looks, there's no way you can look at him and not be able to tell he just had sex upstairs. His hair's a tangled mess, much worse than it was when we got here, yet with that tux on—well, most of the tux on— he still looks like he could walk the red carpet. The women cluster toward his side of the stage. My cheeks flush with heat, certain everyone is noticing. But they're not. They're all entranced by the music. By the rock star standing over them.

I recognize the song, "Tempted by Fate", and smile. This is that first song I heard at the first show I was forced to attend. I hated it then. Now, his voice melts me. His gaze sets me on fire. And just thinking about his touch is enough to send another shiver through me.

I watch him with pride. His talent, the charisma he possesses on stage, it blows me away. He's my rock star. And our world tour has only just begun.

Now that you've gotten a taste of Devon Stone and his dysfunctional train wreck of a life, see what happens when he meets Olivia Margot.

Sweet, neurotic Olivia comes with a heartbreaking past, and the last thing she anticipated when she took a job working for the Stones was the unmistakable spark between her and the black sheep of the Stone empire.

The four book series is told from Olivia's point-of-view, and is available now at all major retailers. Turn the page for a sample!

THE LUST LIST: DEVON STONE

FIRST TASTE

MIRA BAILEE

NoMi Press

Chapter One

I start the morning on a promising note—a full-blown panic attack with a side of desperation.

"Maddie!"

I rush across the living room to the other bedroom in our little apartment. This old place was the best we could afford on our measly incomes in this part of Los Angeles, but we've done our best to spruce it up: scrubbed mildew from the floorboards, strategically placed rugs over the worst of the carpet stains, and I even dedicated my unemployed free time to DIY projects I found online to decorate the bland, beige walls. I'm certain this place is the nicest unit in the building. I mean, Mr. Harrison downstairs has been bitching for months about a two-foot hole in his bathroom wall. Never mind the fact he doesn't want to admit he caused the damage after the Kings lost in overtime. Yeah, this place isn't *that* bad.

But who cares about the state of our apartment when my heart is threatening to escape through my ribs...and my breakfast is threatening to escape through my throat?

Deep breaths.

The jittery feeling persists while I knock on my roommate, Maddie's, door. It swings open with the lightest touch. Her room is dark, and I can hear soft snores coming from the bed.

"Maddie. Wake up. I need you," I say, shaking her foot that hangs out from under the cover.

She groans and rolls over, croaking out an unintelligible slur of words. "It's too early, Olivia. Get the hell out."

My hand goes to my belly, trying to soothe the nauseous feeling. "It's almost noon," I say, tripping over a bag as I walk to the window and pull aside the thick blackout curtains. Harsh sunlight bursts through the thin glass; one of the panes is cracked. Maddie's room illuminates to show off the details that reflect her personality. Dirty laundry strewn about the floor and fast food containers on every surface compete with the intricate silk scarves she has draped over lamps and the string of white Christmas lights woven around the curly iron of her headboard. Maddie is Bohemian-chic meets messy-frat-boy.

In her defense, she does work long hours late into the night bartending at Brecken's Sports Pub. She brings home enough money to help the charity case that is yours truly, covering the rent while I continue my unsuccessful hunt for a job. I'm eternally grateful for her, and I swear I leave her alone most mornings. But today's an important one, and I need Maddie's help.

She's sitting up, assembling her wavy blond hair in a knot on top of her head. Aside from the wreck she resembles when she first wakes up, Maddie is hot—like some perfect combination of classy Academy Award winner and a golden-haired Sports Illustrated swimsuit model, both of which she'd die to be.

"What's wrong?" she asks.

"I need you to help me get dressed."

"Seriously?" She flops back down in bed.

Okay, yes. That sounds pathetic. I'll admit it. But my grandmother has better style than I do, and my closet's filled with clothes that are either worn out from over-washing or two sizes too small. Since my broke ass can't do anything to change what's in there, I have to rely on Maddie—and her talent for making me into a better version of myself—to get me looking like the ideal candidate for Platinum Planning's newest assistant to the head event planner himself, Mr. Greg Keenly. If I land this job, I'll finally make enough money to take care of myself *and* pay Maddie back for everything she's done for me.

"Please. I'm going to end up late if I don't figure this out now, and all I have are ill-fitting, ugly-ass adult clothes."

"You *are* an adult."

"Sure. But I'm twenty-two, and nothing I own looks like it came from the twenty-first century. I need to look good—better than good."

Maddie stumbles out of bed and follows me back to my room. She takes one glance at the outfits laying on my bed—a faded, blue pant-suit and a dress that would better fit a twelve-year-old. Her burst of laughter confirms I need help, and I'm not even offended.

"I told you."

"What's it for? Is it a date? Oh, please tell me it's a date. You so desperately need to get laid. You—"

"It's a job interview."

Maddie's shoulders drop, losing some of her temporary excitement. Of course she would be more worried about me dating than working. My last boyfriend, Bryce, and I broke up over a year ago, and I haven't bothered looking for anyone new. It's too stressful. Dating, the expectations, the whole act of coming across like perfect girlfriend material. More often than not, it just makes me sick. Literally. Being single has its perks. Sure, I'm missing out on potentially decent sex—a momentary relief from my own neurotic nuances, quiet time for my constantly worrying mind. But along with the sex comes the overanalyzing and suspicions and the arguments caused by both. In the end, the guy gets sick of it fast, and I can't blame him. It's much easier to remain single.

Maddie leaves the room only to return a minute later carrying a black dress. She holds it out for me, but I'm skeptical.

"Does that really convey professional—"

"You'll be hot. But not slutty. Put it on." She thrusts it out again, and I take it.

I go to our shared bathroom to change, doing a double take when I see my reflection in the mirror.

"Damn." I can admit this dress gives the right impression. My dark hair frames my face before cascading over my shoulders, detracting from the obvious cleavage this dress gives me. It's formfitting and low-cut but in a way that says 'professional businesswoman' and not 'amateur stripper'. I may even be able to play off confidence if I can get control over the nervous ache in my stomach.

In my room, Maddie is half asleep on my bed. My little square of home is much cleaner than hers but holds little personality. She lifts a hand to point at the side table that holds a simple, white lamp and my charging cell phone. "It was buzzing. I turned it off."

"That means it's time to go." I slip into black flats—no way do I want to deal with heels when I'm feeling all shaky. I'm reaching for my phone when I see Maddie glaring at me. "What?"

"You set an alarm to tell you when to leave?"

"And when to wake up. When to get ready. And a half dozen others to keep me on time today." I grab my purse, unplug my phone, and pull up the map with the directions already routed out. "You shouldn't be surprised."

"I just thought you were working on being less...obsessed with order. Didn't Dr. Shannon—"

"I've gotten better." My therapist has been working on helping me let go of minor control issues in an effort to help me deal with some of the bigger ones. Lately, we've been working on time and my tendency to have everything planned out by the minute. My handy alarms keep me on track, but she says they make me too dependent on outside forces. Days when I'm not busy, I do okay leaving my comfort zone—turning off the alarms and ignoring the clocks—but anticipating today triggered the panic, so I had to give in. Just today. "I see her later. I'll let her know I've been bad."

Maddie sighs, "You're going to be great. Whatever the job is."

"Thank you." I rush over to give her a hug, knowing I need to be in my car in the next thirty seconds. "And thank you for this." I gesture at my dress. "Love you, best friend."

I leave the room as she rolls over in my bed, and I suspect she's not going to bother going back to her own.

Twenty minutes later, when I should be pulling up to the Platinum Planning office, I'm, instead, parked at the security gate of some ritzy housing complex. The guard approaches my window, and I'm not sure what to do next.

"Olivia Margot," I say. "I'm here for an interview at 214 N. Holloway Court."

This guy is inspecting me up and down, a smug grin forming on his face. He's huge—I'm talking Incredible Hulk's nephew huge. He'd tower about two feet over my five-two frame, and I imagine he has to be cautious when hugging his loved ones so as not to accidentally strangle them. His tan skin glistens from a layer of sweat, yet the heat doesn't seem to faze him as he leans down by my window. I shrink into my seat.

"You must be here to see the old man then. He's clearly got a type with you women..."

He's not so subtle as he glances at my chest, and I suddenly remember the low cut dress. Wait. What? Does he think I'm here as a hooker or something? It's midday...on a Monday. Who—?

I fumble to defend myself. "No. I—uh—that's not. I'm here for something else. A real interview. For a *job*."

His smile proves he doesn't believe me, and he steps back from my car. "Have a good day, ma'am. Good luck with that job."

He presses a button inside the little, brick guard station, and the massive gate, adorned with a big letter 'S', swings open. I try to slow my pulse as I follow the only road that leads the way in. *Relax and pretend you're going to the beach. Just focus on the scenery.* The narrow road is lined with tall, meticulously pruned hedges, and beyond them, I can see the tops of palm trees and evergreens. There aren't any houses or side roads or... This isn't a neighborhood. It's one person's property.

The road—driveway—curves up ahead, and as I get closer I see the scene open up before me. A vast, green lawn seems to appear out of nowhere, and the driveway transitions from gray concrete to a mosaic of bricks and stones. It forms a loop at the end, winding its way around a marble fountain, putting on a water show for no audience. In the distance, the ocean meets the horizon. There's nothing but blue out there, but even that secluded chunk of the world—from the depths of the water straight up into the sky above—doesn't seem to compare to the massive mansion standing before me.

"Holy shit."

Chapter Two

I'd like to say I don't end up driving three times around the fancy fountain, trying to figure out the appropriate place to park, but yeah, that's me. I finally notice where the driveway extends to one side of the house, and I pull up behind the only other car I see. It's a freshly waxed, black Lexus—a shiny onyx compared to the faded denim-color of my twenty-year-old Saturn. I get out of the car but can't bring myself to take a step closer to the monstrous structure in front of me. Where am I? Whose house is this? Glancing at the screen of my phone, I have eight minutes to go. My nerves are still too unreliable to go inside early. I need to feel relaxed enough to know I won't go in and vomit right in front of my interviewer.

It's quiet out here with the peaceful sounds of the Pacific Ocean coming from the frigging backyard. The soothing rhythm of the crashing waves draws me to it, and I walk around the back corner of the house to see what, I assume, is a spectacular sight.

Like something out of a dream, the view is unimaginable. A stone patio leads to an infinity pool that appears to drop straight into the ocean. An iron, spiral staircase leads the way to a second level upstairs, and beyond that one, other similar balconies extend out the back of the house. I'm jealous of whoever gets to leave their room and immediately enter a paradise. I try to stay out of direct view of the enormous windows spanning the walls along the back of the mansion as I make my way closer to the far end of the pool. A short, hidden stairway brings you down to the beach level where these people seem to have this part of Mother Nature all to themselves.

I'd do anything to live in a place like this. I don't need to even go inside. I'd be happy pitching a tent right there on the sand. Fall asleep to the whooshing sound of the water. Wake up to the salty, clean air of a new day...

There. Now I feel at ease, like I can handle today.

"Are you lost?"

I almost jump out of my skin as I whirl around to see who's interrupted my moment of serenity.

One look at him, and I'm right back to square one. My throat catches, and I feel my palms clamming up.

This guy is unbelievably gorgeous. Tall, dark hair, piercing blue eyes, and he's dressed like...like he belongs here. I sure as hell don't, and I'm feeling that certainty increase by the second. If this is his house, then he figured out life long before me. I just graduated with a bachelor's in Hospitality and can't snag a job to save my life. I end up with shitty, part-time gigs just to scrape by. Food service instead of a flourishing career. A run-down apartment instead of a... I look around at this magnificent mansion and the beautiful man standing before me.

He's holding a suit jacket, and the navy blue tie around his neck is loose and framing a white dress shirt, its top button undone. Please tell me this is Mr. Keenly. I'll do my best not to screw up if I can just get a chance to work for this guy.

But who am I kidding? I'm not even talking to him now as he stands there with a confused expression on his face.

"Um...sorry. No, I'm—uh—actually here to meet with Mr. Keenly. Is that you?"

"God, no. That's the asshole planning Saturday's party. You working for him?" He checks me out, furrowing his brow, and I'm reminded of the creep at the front gate.

Of course he's not a party planner. He's got to be a model or something. I'm an idiot for asking. "No. Not yet anyway. I'm supposed to have an interview... But I may have changed my mind."

As inviting as he is in appearance, he seems to be tense. Maybe even angry. His fist clenches a phone, and he pushes his loose hair away from his face. However it had been styled this morning, it's disheveled now, like he just got done fighting with someone or having sex... A vulgar image flashes across my mind. Him. Me. My back up against a wall.

Snap out of it, O.

Is he mad at me? Did I insult him? I check my phone to see I have two minutes left. It'll buzz at 12:30, yet I still feel the need to double check in case I set the wrong alarm or my phone decided to malfunction. You never know.

Right now, I want to flee. Forget the interview. I can't stand out here any longer making an ass out of myself. I can just leave. Maddie can help me with rent...again, and I'm sure I can find a job at some chain restaurant or a motel needing an overnight concierge. Something low-key, simple. I'm certain if I stick around, what's waiting for me inside will be anything but low-key *or* simple.

I realize from an outside perspective, I'm just standing here, fidgeting and staring at the tan skin peeking out from under my hot stranger's shirt collar. He's clearly noticed, and a mischievous grin replaces his former scowl.

"So you changed your mind? Want to bail?" He glances up toward a window and returns his gaze to me. "If you need an excuse to get out of the interview, I can fill your schedule with something else..."

What is he talking about? He doesn't even know me. Is it the dress? Dammit, I look easy, don't I? Thanks a lot, Maddie. But what kind of guy just puts it all out there like that?

I turn and start toward the door right as my phone begins vibrating. If I have to choose between responding to that obvious come-on and dealing with an awkward job interview, then I'll go find Mr. Keenly now.

"So what's your name?"

This guy is walking alongside of me, not taking my silence as a hint.

"Huh? I have to go in now."

"I just asked your name. If you can't answer that then, damn, this interview's going to suck for you."

I laugh but try to stifle it. I shouldn't encourage him. I'm getting some serious weird vibes from him, like he's used to getting anything he wants. With a face and body like that, I can imagine it's the truth.

"My name's Olivia. Margot."

"Well, Olivia. Good luck to you." We've reached the huge double doors at the front of the house, and he opens one for me. "I'm sure I'll see you around."

We step inside, and the look on his face shifts. His eyes turn cold, and he marches upstairs. So he *is* mad. But, thankfully, not at me. I'm not sure I'd want to be on his bad side. Then again, I'm not sure I want to be on his good side either. His presence is overwhelming, and he demands attention. I imagine dating him would be exhausting.

Dating? No. I'm here for an interview.

"Miss Margot, correct?" A stubby, well-dressed man is waiting in a doorway to my right. I rush over realizing I may officially be late thanks to Mr. No-Name.

I reach out my hand to shake his. This guy will be much easier to talk to now that I've survived the encounter with that anonymous male model. *You've got this girl. Now kick some interview ass.*

"Thank you so much for meeting with me."

"Yes, I see you found the place alright—"

"This is bullshit!" Stomping footsteps interrupt us as Mr. Hunk follows an older, white-haired man back down the stairs. The old man is dressed in a robe—in the middle of the day—and seems to be nursing a glass of scotch, but I can see from their scowls alone, they're father and son. So I assume he's *the* old man according to the gate guard. "You and Kaidan know what you're doing, and you're screwing me over in the meantime."

He follows him into another room across the foyer, slamming the door behind them. Their arguing continues, muffled through the walls.

Mr. Keenly rolls his eyes. "Let's speak in here where it's quieter."

The Lust List

The Lust List - Take Your Pick

They're the world's sexiest bachelors. The men of *ScandalLust* mag's infamous Lust List are young, wealthy, and, oh, did we mention? *Hot.*

When scandal follows them everywhere, there's no hiding from the cameras. They're irresistible, insatiable—and talented in all the right ways. Every woman wants them. But these playboys won't be easy to catch...

The Lust List

Devon Stone

by Mira Bailee

FIRST TASTE
SECOND CHANCES
THIRD DEGREE
FOUR LETTERS

AVAILABLE NOW

Acknowledgments

Another series is complete, and I have some amazing people to thank for it: my editor, Nicole Bailey, who makes all my words much prettier; Najla Qamber, who designs the sexiest book covers; Nova Raines, who took on the challenge of co-authoring this massive series with me; and all my readers, who make this adventure worthwhile—

Now onto the next one!

About Mira Bailee

Mira Bailee, a beer-brewing librarian, has been writing leisurely, scholarly, and professionally for the past twenty years.

While she's always maintained a high standard of chaos in her daily routine, *The Lust List* allows her to pass on some of her hectic lifestyle to her characters. Her storytelling balances humor and pleasure with sincerity and conflict, providing a wild ride of human emotions.

In the past she studied filmmaking and screenwriting and determined what goes on behind the scenes is just as tantalizing as what's seen in front of the camera. This revelation is the basis for her inspiration for *The Lust List*.